The Wishing Sisters
and Other Forest Tales

by

Maggie Holman

Published by Run Jump Jive

First published in the United Kingdom in 2008
by Run Jump Jive
PO Box 3876, Berkshire SL5 0WD
runjumpjive@yahoo.co.uk

ISBN 978-0-9561181-0-3

A CIP catalogue record for this book
is available from the British Library

Cover photograph by John Holman
with permission of The Forestry Commission

Text Design and Typeset by Run Jump Jive
Printed and bound in Great Britain by
Blue Mushroom Limited
85 Guildford Street, Chertsey, Surrey KT16 9AS

For Jennifer,
still my 'Wishing Sister'

Contents

The Wishing Sisters

November 26th 1888

At eight o'clock this morning, my husband Jacob left me. He didn't mean to, but he went anyway. No-one could have seen it coming - a collapse in the main pit, everyone buried. It was a little boy who told us. He ran all the way across the fields until he reached our little row of houses. Poor thing! We bathed his little feet where they were cut and blistered, and he lay back against my neighbour Amelia's garden wall and told us all, in short breathless sentences, the terrible news. The rescue was quick. One thing about mining accidents is there are always other miners there to help straight away. By nightfall they had everyone out - forty-two in all - and all of them dead. The worst disaster for years, it said in the local paper. They brought Jacob home and laid him out on our kitchen table. He was a shadow of his living self. His pale face seemed wrapped in sleep, and while I sat with him that night - for I wasn't afraid - I felt that at any moment I could reach out and shake him, and he'd wake up. But I knew there was no waking up for Jacob. Never again. And all I could think about was the times I'd woken in the night and whispered 'I love you' into his ear as he slept, and had I done this enough times? Had he gone on his final journey, with forty-one souls in tow, knowing how much I adored him?

December 1st 1888

The mining company wasted no time. I couldn't stay in our home now that I was alone. These cottages are for miners and their families. The letter reminded me when it arrived, the day after Jacob's funeral. So I have done the only thing I can, with reluctance, and written to my brother Michael, to ask for a room in his home.

December 3rd 1888

What a speedy reply came from Michael! Instead of writing back to me, he arrived today with his horse and cart, accompanied by his youngest daughter, Martha. Together we packed up my belongings and set off for the farm. I have not seen Michael for some years, even though we had always been close. He and his wife Sarah live a good distance away, on a farm Michael saved hard to buy before he proposed to her. The year they married, the snow fell so badly the night before that Jacob and I were trapped in our home, unable to attend. Michael understood our lack of control over such things as weather and travel, but my new sister-in-law was not so forgiving, and never spoke to us again after we missed her special day. This was the reason for my reluctance to write now. I lived in a happy home with Jacob, and I now travelled with trepidation to take a place under Sarah's roof, where in spite of Michael's cheerfulness, I expected to find tension.

Sarah was waiting at the door as we pulled up in the farmyard. She greeted me civilly but frostily, and showed me around the house while Michael and two of his farm workers took my things to the spare room. We all sat down to dinner at the huge kitchen table that evening - Michael, Sarah, my two young nieces Martha and Elizabeth, and myself - and everyone ate in stony silence. Afterwards I went to my room, looked at my wedding photograph in a frame on the bedside table, and wept into my pillow.

December 6th 1888

I have been here at the farm for three days. My two nieces are delightful. Their company cheers me up and distracts me from my thoughts. Michael is usually absent until the evening, out on the land, and I am trying my best to endear myself to Sarah with offers of help around the house and with the girls. I get the impression that I cannot win, as Sarah seems happiest when she refuses my offers, as if I am intruding into her control of the domestic domain. I think this may be used against me at some later date.

December 7th 1888

Last night I had the strangest experience. I woke with a start. The clock on the wall said three o'clock, and I listened to the darkness, wondering what had awoken me. After a few minutes I heard a sound. It was the distinct, unmistakable sound of a woman crying. Carefully I got up, put on my dressing gown and lit the oil lamp that stood next to my bed. I opened my bedroom door, hoping not to disturb anyone with its creak, and looked up and down the landing. The farmhouse is big but not sprawling, and in a few minutes I was able to explore the whole of the upstairs area. No-one else was about, investigating the sound, and I set off downstairs to search there. Again, I found nothing. The crying gradually subsided, and I set off back to my room. As I turned at the top of the stairwell, I jumped in fright, and then relaxed, when I realised it was Sarah standing in the moonlight.
"What are you doing?" she asked.
"I heard someone crying - a woman - and I went to investigate."
"Impossible. There's no other woman here. Only you and me."
"Well, it was probably a dream," I said as I stepped past her.
Just then, Martha opened her door, rubbing her eyes sleepily.
"There - now you've disturbed the children. I'll thank you not to start making a habit of wandering about in the night."

Sarah hushed Martha back into her room. She closed the door behind her, and left me standing in the passageway, trying to make sense of what I'd heard.

December 8th 1888

This afternoon I was sitting in my room, reading. I looked up to see Elizabeth standing in the doorway. I smiled at her.

"What is it?"

Elizabeth hesitated and then walked across the room. She stood by my chair and looked around. Something seemed to be bothering her.

"Elizabeth - is something wrong?"

Finally she spoke.

"I heard the crying last night," she said quietly.

"You did? Then I didn't imagine it."

"And I've heard it every night since you came."

I stared at Elizabeth.

"Did you ever hear the crying before I came to stay?"

She nodded a 'no'.

"It was you, Aunt Hannah," she blurted out.

"What do you mean?"

"You were crying last night. You've been crying every night since you came. I can hear you in my room."

I froze, unsure what to say.

"But it sounded like it was coming from somewhere else," I protested. "I couldn't find out where."

"No," Elizabeth said firmly. "The crying is inside you."

She turned and walked out of the room, and I was left wondering why a small child would say such a strange thing.

December 9th 1888

In the last few days, I have taken to walking in the woods on the edge of the farmyard. The trees remind me of the area around my own home, and I believe there is nowhere on earth that gives a person the sense of peace and solitude that I get when I walk in these woods alone. At this time of year the bare, leafless trees, and the still, dark surfaces of secluded ponds, and the eerie mist that hangs over everything, all combine to create a picture that mirrors my sadness. I think it is helping me when I walk deep into the trees, sit by the still water, and remember those memories that only belong to me, and no-one else. I need to do this, because I don't know what else to do. I feel so alone.

Imagine my surprise, then, today, when I turned a corner in the path and saw someone - a woman walking alone, like me - in the distance. I laughed to myself afterwards, because I didn't expect to see anyone in so remote a place, and the sight had made me jump. I watched carefully, out of view, as she strolled away. I don't think she saw me, because she didn't react as if she saw me, and she carried on, disappearing eventually into the trees.

December 12th 1888

I feel more and more miserable here at the farm. This morning I was lying awake in bed, having awoken early, and I could hear Michael and Sarah arguing. They were arguing about me.

"Leave her alone, Sarah. You can be so cruel at times," I heard Michael say.

"I wasn't sure she should come here, and I was right," Sarah was shouting back.

"Hannah needs time. She's hurting."

"How do you know? She doesn't really talk to us, and she hardly helps around the place, when she knows how busy I am with the house and the children."

I knew that would happen. I knew Sarah wanted to paint a poor picture of me.

"Have you ever considered, Sarah, putting yourself in her position for a moment? What if I went out today and had an accident somewhere and didn't come back? How would you feel?"

I listened for Sarah's reply, and it didn't come. I knew Michael would be hurt by the silence.

"I'm not listening to your moaning again, Sarah. My sister is welcome here, in my home!"

With that, he left, slamming the door behind him.

Later that morning, Sarah ignored me as I crossed the kitchen to go for my walk. This time, I walked a different route, deeper into the woods than usual. Eventually I came across a quiet pond, one I'd not seen before. Its surface was peaceful and still, and I found a makeshift seat on an uprooted tree that lay next to the path. As I stared at the water, I knew I was going to cry. I miss Jacob so much. He used to make me laugh, and now there was no laughter in my life, except from my young nieces as they played. Should I cry? Will I feel better?

Just then, something distracted me. I noticed a movement off in the trees on the other side of the pond. Gradually the movement took form, as I realised it was the same woman I'd seen a couple of days ago. Quickly I jumped up and hid behind a large tree. I didn't want her to see me, although I didn't know why. When I peeped around the edge of the tree, I saw that she had stopped at the water's edge and was looking across, straight at me. Did she know I was hiding from her? I moved back behind the tree again and waited. I wanted her to go away. These are my woods. My walks. My space. My grief. Slowly I edged round the tree again.

She was still there, still watching. Then, out of the blue, she waved. At me! I didn't wave back. I hid back behind the tree and looked around, in a panic. What did she want? What did she want with me? I waited and waited for what seemed like an age, and when I looked again, she was gone.

December 14th 1888

Tonight Michael, Sarah and myself were sitting in the kitchen. It was late, about eight-thirty. We had eaten our evening meal and washed up. The children were in bed. Michael sat by the fire, reading. Sarah and I were sitting together at the table, mending the rips and tears that constantly appear in Michael's work clothes.

There was a knock at the front door. It was a quiet, gentle knock, and we all three just heard it. Sarah looked across quizzically at Michael, who glanced up at the clock on the mantelpiece. He got up and went out into the hallway, while Sarah and I remained seated. I listened as Michael opened the front door, spoke in a muffled voice saying something I couldn't catch, and then closed the door again. Michael returned to the kitchen, and following behind him was the woman I had seen on my walks.

"This is my wife Sarah, and my sister Hannah."

The woman smiled at us both. I looked at her properly. She was a little bit older than me, I'd say, and she had a calm, relaxed air about her that was missing here at the farm.

"I'm very pleased to meet you both," she said.

It was the first time I had heard her voice, and it sounded friendly and kind.

"Sarah - this is Ellen. She's called to see Hannah. Can you light the lamps in the drawing room, please, so that they can sit in there, and have some privacy."

I was surprised to hear Michael's words, but also pleased. However, I saw my sister-in-law stiffen next to me, and her face fell into her frostiest expression yet. The drawing room was reserved for special occasions such as Christmas, and as such was left largely unused. I knew that she resented Michael's request, and that she was offended by the idea that she was being left out of something happening in her own home. She stood up quickly, looked at Michael and then left the room. Ever cheerful, Michael broke the silence.

"So, how do you know my sister?" he asked Ellen.

"We've seen each other when we've been out walking in the woods. I thought I'd call and say hello."

"Good," said Michael, enthusiastically. He looked across at me.

"Some different company will do you good, Hannah."

Just then, as if on cue, Sarah returned.

"I've lit the lamps, Hannah, and I've also laid a fire. It may be a little cold in there to begin with."

"Thank you very much," Ellen replied.

She turned expectantly towards me, and I stood up and led the way. The drawing room was warm and cheerful. It did not have the same austere air that existed around the rest of the farmhouse.

"Please, have a seat," I motioned to the pair of armchairs that were placed on either side of the now roaring fire. Ellen sat down in one, while I sat down in the other. At first there was an uncomfortable silence, and then we both spoke at once.

"I hope you don't mind me........." Ellen began.

"It's nice of you to..............." I began at the same time.

We both stopped and laughed.

"I'd seen you a few times out in the woods, always on your own," Ellen continued. "I don't have anyone to walk with either, so I t h o u g h t I'd call and see if you wanted to meet, and we could keep each other company."

"I'd like that very much," I replied. I don't know why I was suddenly so sure of making arrangements with someone I'd only just met, but it seemed the natural thing to do.

"It's a lonely place, out here, for people who are feeling lonely," Ellen commented.

"Yes, it is. Do you live far from here?" I asked.

"Not far. I have a house on the edge of the woods, down the track behind here."

"Oh, yes. I know the track you mean."

"Would you like to go for a walk tomorrow morning?"

I paused and looked at Ellen before answering her.

"Yes, I'd like that."

Ellen stood up and pulled her bonnet on.

"That's settled, then. No more solitary walks for either of us. I'll meet you by the farmyard gate. About ten?"

"Yes, alright. Thank you."

Ellen smiled.

"No, thank you. You're helping me."

I walked Ellen to the front door and watched her disappear into the dark. What a strange thing to say - I was helping her. What did she mean? And what was stranger, why didn't she ask me anything? She didn't ask why I was at the farm, or how long I'd been there, or anything about me. I returned to the kitchen, where Michael and Sarah sat together. They both turned their heads to look as I came in.

"Ellen lives round the back, on the edge of the woods."

"Funny. Can't say I've ever seen her around the place," said Michael. "Still, she seems pleasant. Bit of company for you, Hannah, on your walks."

Sarah said nothing.

December 15th 1888

This morning I woke early. When I looked out of my window, the farmyard was bathed in an eerie mist. The sky was pale and gloomy. It was too early to be up yet, so I curled back up under my blankets and went back to sleep. It was then that I had a strange dream. I dreamt that I was in a boat on Cannop Pond. I was with Ellen, and someone else was rowing us along. Everything was so vivid. I remember looking down into the water and seeing the fish and the weed in the depths below. The boat glided slowly, travelling away from the bank. Then I woke up.

I met Ellen as we'd arranged. At precisely ten o'clock, she was waiting for me by the gate. We walked into the woods, chatting as we went. I've decided not to mention Jacob to Ellen. That memory is too private.

December 21st 1888

For the last few days, I have met Ellen every day and gone for a walk with her. She is pleasant company, and I find her easy to spend time with. At the same time, every night, I have had the same dream about the boat. Sometimes we are getting into the boat, at the water's edge. Sometimes it is gliding slowly through the water. This morning, I brought the dreams up in our conversation as we walked.

"Dreams have a purpose. You know that, don't you, Hannah?"

"I always thought they helped you sort things out, things from the real, awake world that need organising in our heads."

"Possibly," Ellen continued. "But I think dreams do much more than that. They tell us things, help us with things, prepare us for things."

I looked at her as we walked.

"For instance, what do you think your dream is about, when we are in the boat together? And why do you keep having the same dream?"

I laughed.

"I have no idea. I was hoping you might be able to tell me."

Ellen stopped and suddenly looked serious.

"It could be that we are going on a journey, you and I, that will take us to a new place, and things will be different."

"What, a journey across a pond in a boat? Where to?"

"Don't take it all too literally, Hannah. Journeys take all sorts of forms."

"You're confusing me," I laughed.

"Then stop thinking about it. Don't want you being confused. You'll get us lost."

We both laughed and walked on. We stopped at the gates to the farm.

"I woke up and heard a woman crying, just one time, when I first came here," I suddenly blurted out. "My niece says she hears the crying every night. She says it's me. Is that a dream?"

11

Ellen looked carefully at me.

"I don't know. I'm not there."

I felt foolish and looked away.

"You know, Hannah, things happen that we don't expect or understand. They happen to us all the time. We can't always understand or explain them, but they still happen. Do you know what I mean?"

I felt tears coming to my eyes.

"I have to go inside," I said, and hurried away.

December 23rd 1888

The last two days have been quite strange. Every day I've met Ellen and enjoyed my walk and my conversation with her. And every time I've fallen asleep, I've dreamed about the boat; Ellen and I, in the boat, drifting slowly across the pond. At the end of our walk this morning, I mentioned these dreams again. Ellen smiled.

"You really shouldn't worry," she said. "Listen - tomorrow is Christmas Eve. Would you like to come over to my house and stay for Christmas Day?"

I looked at Ellen. Of course part of me knew that Christmas was looming. Martha and Elizabeth were excited and had written their letters to Father Christmas, each of them squealing in delight when the envelopes shot up the chimney. But part of me hadn't realised that it was nearly here. Part of me didn't want Christmas to come at all, when Jacob wasn't here to share it.

"Thank you for inviting me, but I don't know if I could do that. Christmas - this Christmas - will be.........difficult."

In all our conversations, I had still never mentioned Jacob, and Ellen had never asked me about my life before I came to the farm.

"I know it will be difficult," Ellen suddenly said.

I looked at her, puzzled.

"You'll probably offend your sister-in-law further by coming to stay with me, but I think it would be a good idea. Please say you'll come."

December 24th 1888

This morning I broke the news, as we all sat in the kitchen before chores started, that I had been invited to spend Christmas with Ellen, and that I was going to go. Ellen was coming to collect me after our evening meal. There was a pause, then Michael came across and hugged me.

"You must do what you feel is best for you," he said. "This first Christmas will be the hardest."

He smiled. I looked across at Sarah and knew she wasn't pleased. I wished at that moment that she could see herself and the way she did things from outside, so that she might relax a little, warm a little, and really be like the sister I need right now.

"I have some small presents for you all," I offered.

"Then we'll exchange our presents this evening before you go," Michael said positively. "Won't we, Sarah."

"Yes. I'd like that," Sarah suddenly said.

Our evening meal was less austere and silent than in previous weeks. We laughed and joked as we ate, mostly due to my brother's efforts, and then we exchanged our gifts and played games with the girls. This time, when there was a quiet knock at the front door, we all knew it was Ellen. She joined us in the kitchen while I said goodbye to everyone, and everyone greeted her warmly.

"Well - Merry Christmas, Hannah," Sarah said.

I appreciated that she seemed sincere and reached out to give her a hug. Afterwards, Ellen and I left together and walked along the lane at the back of the farm to her cottage. As I followed Ellen up the garden path to her front door, I didn't know what to expect, but here was a bright cheerful front room! A cosy bed for me to spend Christmas in! Lots of decorations! I know that as I fall asleep on this Christmas Eve, here in Ellen's home, that I will have a lovely time here tomorrow.

December 25th 1888

It is the early hours, still dark and black. I'm sitting up in bed and I am afraid. I've had the strangest dream. At least I think it was a dream. In my dream, I was asleep in this bed in Ellen's house, when suddenly the bedroom door opened and Ellen came quietly in. She was carrying an oil lamp which was turned down low, but still managed to throw weird shadows across the room. I watched lazily as Ellen put the lamp down on the small table next to my bed and then sat down on the bed itself, next to me. She knew I was awake and she looked straight at me.

"I want to tell you something, Hannah. It's very important."

She seemed to pause, watching my reaction, before she continued.

"I want to tell you that I know where Jacob is. And more important still, I want to show you where he is."

I remember feeling, in my dreamlike state, that this seemed perfectly reasonable and I didn't feel the need to question Ellen's words.

"Just watch, and then remember," she whispered.

Ellen raised her hand and held it out, the fingers stretched out flat and the palm turned upwards. She sat like this for some time without moving, while the shadows continued to flicker in the lamplight. Then - suddenly - a tiny light appeared. It seemed to rise from Ellen's upturned palm, and then it floated up and away into the air. A second light appeared, then another, and then more and more, until the air was filled with tiny lights that floated slowly around us. They all seemed to come deliberately from Ellen's hand, as if she were responsible for their release, and they gave off such feelings of light and peace and comfort that I wanted to cry. After a few minutes in this static place, the lights began to fade. They grew dimmer and dimmer, floating closer and closer to Ellen again, until eventually they were extinguished altogether, leaving us sitting in the shadows. Ellen turned to me and smiled.

"Goodnight," was all she said, and she got up from the bed, picked up the lamp again and left the room, closing the door quietly behind her. Like I said, I think it was a dream.

This morning, when I awoke, last night's disturbing dream stayed with me. It made me afraid and confused when I thought of that strange memory of Ellen sitting on my bed, surrounded by the weird lights that emerged from her upturned palm. I dressed and went downstairs to discover Ellen was already up, dressed and peeling vegetables. She turned and smiled at me, and I handed her my small Christmas gift - a scarf with a pattern that I had embroidered myself.

"Merry Christmas, Hannah. And thank you, this is lovely."

I watched Ellen as she placed the scarf on the chair and continued to peel the vegetables. I tried to believe that everything was normal, but I sensed that Ellen could tell that something was wrong. However, I was completely unprepared for what she said next.

"I'm afraid I couldn't wrap my gift to give you, Hannah."

"Don't worry. I wasn't expecting anything."

Ellen laughed a little.

"No, Hannah. You misunderstand me. As if I wasn't going to give you a gift! It just doesn't need to be wrapped; it isn't a solid thing. In fact, I gave you part of it already."

I stared at Ellen, even more confused.

"My Christmas gift, Hannah, is the things I want to say to you, when you need them most. I started to tell you these things last night, in your dream."

Dumbfounded, I sank into one of the chairs, full of mixed emotions; fear, confusion, and in a strange way, relief. I responded quietly.

"I dreamt that you came into my room, that you were surrounded by lights, that you told me you knew where Jacob was."

"That's right," Ellen replied, almost matter-of-factly.

"But I've never spoken to you about Jacob. How could you know about him? Did someone else tell you? Sarah? Or my brother Michael?"

Ellen suddenly became very serious.

"Jacob told me everything."

I jumped to my feet.

"Enough," I shouted. "Enough of this talk. Jacob died in a mining accident. You never knew him, Ellen. Stop talking like this at once!"

Ellen seemed frustrated. She pulled up a chair and sat in front of me. For a moment she didn't speak, and hot tears sprang into my eyes.

"I miss Jacob terribly," I sobbed. "And I have no-one to talk to."

"But can't you see, that's why I came?" Ellen said quietly.

"To support you."

"But how?"

"This will seem very strange, Hannah, but please listen to me."

I continued to cry as Ellen leaned forward towards me.

"Be still now. Just listen. I didn't meet Jacob until after he died. He came to me because he was worried abut you, being so suddenly on your own."

I wept openly now.

"He knows that you sat with him all night, when they brought him home, and he's around you all the time, only you can't see him."

My crying slowed a little as I felt Ellen lean further still towards me.

"And now, Hannah, I want you to relax, breathe slowly, and open your mind. I'm going to take your hands in mine and give you the last part of my gift."

I closed my eyes and felt Ellen take my hands gently in hers. Suddenly, my head seemed to fill with a whirlwind of images coming at me from all directions, coming and going, mingling and merging, dissolving again. Ellen was filling my head with a collage of memories, and Jacob was in every image. There we were, walking by the river, sitting by the fire, dancing, talking, kissing. I couldn't stop myself smiling through my tears, and then something even stranger happened. I felt Ellen's small delicate hands change to larger, stronger hands; hands I already knew. I opened my eyes, and there was Jacob in front of me, smiling, holding me steady. In a total fright, I snatched my hands away and opened my eyes properly, blinking at the winter sun in Ellen's kitchen. I stood up, stepping back into a corner, and looked around. Ellen and I were the only people there.

"This is evil, Ellen. What are you doing?"

"Trying to help."

"No, you're not. You're trying to frighten me."

"Not at all. Please try to understand. You need to come to terms with what's happened and move on, not feel trapped in a place where every day is the same and things don't move forwards."

I felt myself becoming angry. Instinctively, I saw the sharp knife Ellen had been using earlier to peel the vegetables. It was lying on the table. I sprang across the kitchen in one movement, grabbed the knife and turned to Ellen, pointing the knife at her.

"Calm down, Hannah. I've opened an emotional wound for you, but we have to continue on to the end - see it through."

"No!" I shouted. "Keep away from me! I'm going back to the farm, and you will not stop me, or try to see me there!"

"No, Hannah............"

"Yes. Yes! That's the end of this matter. Jacob was my husband, not yours, and you will not draw yourself into my grief, just to s a t i s f y some need of your own."

Ellen looked resigned.

"Please stay, Hannah," was all she said, but I dropped the knife, ran out of the door without collecting my things, and didn't stop running until I reached the safety of the farmyard gate.

December 26th 1888

When I returned yesterday, neither Michael nor Sarah asked me why I'd returned so abruptly and in such a state. I was relieved not to be questioned, for I now had too much on my mind, and I spent the rest of Christmas Day alone in my room. Later, on Boxing Night, we all sat together in the sitting room. Sarah could play the piano a little, and she sat with the girls, singing together as she played Christmas carols and songs. Michael sat by the fire, reading, and I looked across the scene, happy that they all seemed content together.

A knock at the front door interrupted the peaceful domestic scene. The music round the piano stopped, and everyone listened while Michael went to answer the door. When he came back, he looked at me.
    "Ellen is at the door. She wants to speak to you."
I looked at Michael, and with a certainty that surprised me, I simply said "Tell Ellen that I do not wish to speak to her."
    Michael nodded and went out again. I heard muffled voices in a brief exchange, and then the sound of the front door closing. When Michael returned, he sat down and continued to read, while Sarah struck up the introduction to another song.

December 29th 1888

Ellen has called at the farm every day since she first called on Boxing Day. Each time my message to her was the same; this friendship should not continue. I feel so confused about everything, and the dreams are still there. Always the same. Ellen and I, in a boat, gliding though the reeds.

December 30th 1888

This morning Michael and Sarah took the girls to visit their friends who own the farm on the next hill. Michael invited me to go as well, but I declined. At twelve o'clock I heated some stew on the range, and as I glanced out of the kitchen window, I stiffened. Ellen was walking across the farmyard towards the front door. When she disappeared from view, I left the kitchen and stood waiting in the hallway, behind the front door.
    First Ellen knocked quietly. I didn't answer, and I wondered if she knew I was standing so close by. There was a pause, then a second, sharper knock. I crept across the hallway to the stairs and sat on the bottom stair, facing the door. Waiting expectantly, I still jumped when Ellen called out.

"Hannah? If you can hear me, please open the door."

She sounded concerned, almost pleading, and I wasn't sure what to do, so I did nothing. After another pause, Ellen knocked again, and then I watched as an envelope appeared under the door. Next I heard Ellen's footsteps as she walked away. Tonight, when I went to bed, I sat up and turned the envelope over and over. My name was written on the front, and there was no indication of its contents. I decided I had to read it before I went to sleep, and tore the envelope open. It was a short, simple message:

'Dear Hannah,

I'm sorry we've become distant. Please remember the
friendship we found. I so enjoyed our conversations and
our walks in the woods. I'm going to Cannop Pond with
everyone else tomorrow, for the New Year's Day picnic.
I suppose Michael and Sarah will be taking the children.
It's a nice day out. I do hope you'll come. It's so nice on
the water at this time of year.

Your dear friend,
Ellen'

There was no mention of Jacob, or our stressful conversation in the kitchen, or all the conversations we'd had about my dreams. Did I imagine it all? Why was I so unsure?

December 31st 1888

Ellen's letter must have been praying on my mind when I went to sleep last night, because I dreamt again about being in the boat with Ellen, gliding through the water. But this time there was more. As the boat approached the bank side on its return, it suddenly tipped up, and Ellen and I both fell into the water. I woke up with a terrifying image of Ellen floating away and disappearing under the surface, while I struggled to reach her in my wet, heavy dress. Tomorrow I will go to Cannop, because I have a bad feeling. I must tell Ellen about my dream.

January 2nd 1889

Today I'm confined to bed, with plenty of time to contemplate the terrible thing I did yesterday. I can't quite believe it, but I made the events of my dream come true.

I went to Cannop yesterday morning, as I'd planned, with the intention of persuading Ellen not to go out on the water. When I found her in the crowd, she was so pleased to see me, and so excited that I'd come to join her, that she wouldn't hear anything of the concerns I had.

"Come on, Hannah. It's a lovely trip up and down the pond. You'll enjoy it."

Reluctantly I climbed into the boat. Ellen and I were the only passengers, and there was a queue of people waiting their turn. The boat was owned by Old Pete, who would spend the day ferrying people up and down, to make a little money with which to start his New Year.

The scenery was beautiful. The mist gradually rose up off the trees, and the sun reflected off the water. I relaxed a little and tried to enjoy the ride, although I avoided looking down into the deep water below; I'd seen that enough times already. When we reached the bulrushes at the end, and we turned to head back, that's when it happened. I looked across at Ellen and her face said it all. I caught her watching me, and I knew then that everything was real - the crying in the night, the dreams, seeing Jacob on Christmas morning. I realised in that instant that Ellen had been trying to look after me, and I'd been stupid and foolish. What was worse, I was letting Ellen down when it was my turn to look after her. I should never have let her come out in the boat. In a moment of panic, I stood up.

"We have to get back to the bank," I shouted. "It's not safe!"

"Sit down!" shouted Pete. "And sit still! You'll tip us up!"

And that's exactly what happened. As if in slow motion, but really in seconds, I felt the boat tip over, and the three of us were thrown in. I braced myself as I fell, but was still completely unprepared for the icy water. I went under once, and could feel the weeds and the fish around me, before I fought my way back up and burst through the surface, gasping for breath. I struggled in my heavy clothes, which were getting heavier every second, as I saw someone reach to pull Pete safely out. As I tried to tread water, I searched for Ellen. She came up to the surface a few feet away from me, but what was she doing? She was floating away from me, away and under, just like she did in my dream. She wasn't making any effort to swim. Why wasn't she trying to save herself?

"Ellen!" I screamed. "Hang on!"

I managed to kick off my boots, and then laboured against my heavy dress, trying to lift my arms and swim across to where Ellen was sinking fast. Her eyes were closed and she lay back in the water, but when I reached her and grabbed hold of her, she seemed to stir. She opened her eyes and looked at me.

"Leave me be, Hannah," she said quietly. "This was meant to happen."

"What are you talking about?" I shouted, as I held onto her and kicked hard, trying to move us both closer to shore.

"It has to be like this, Hannah. Let me go. You're not supposed to interfere."

With that Ellen pushed hard against me, writhing free of my grip. I didn't expect her to do this, and so she managed to kick away from me again before I could stop her. I resolved to try to reach her again, but suddenly I found myself struggling. My dress seemed to be snagged on something hidden underwater, and I couldn't move. I could only watch, helpless, as Ellen slipped away, calm and serene, eyes closed, into the dark water. I screamed and screamed for help, and then hands grabbed me from behind. Someone pulled and I felt my dress rip free of its underwater trap. I turned to see that it was Michael pulling me from behind, up onto the bank, as I sobbed and screamed for them to find Ellen.

I first woke late this afternoon. To my surprise, Sarah was sitting by my bed, reading. Michael came to see me when Sarah told him I was awake. He brought me some hot soup, for which I was very grateful. I think I'm getting a chill, as I can't seem to keep warm and yet I feel very hot and shivery. I can't get Michael's news out of my mind - that after searching the pond and the banks, they can't find Ellen's body anywhere. I wanted to get up and go to Ellen's cottage, but Michael has advised me not to. He wouldn't tell me why.

January 3rd 1889

This morning I woke early. The sun was just rising and the house was silent. I lay in bed for a long while, watching the sky grow steadily lighter through my open curtains. I got up and stood at the window. In the distance, the trees were covered in their eerie early morning mist. I had been in bed for two days since the accident on the pond, and I decided to go for an early morning walk. I had a feeling that people would disapprove, so I dressed very quietly and crept out of the house. Something was bothering me - something I wanted an answer to. Outside, the grass felt crisp under my feet as I left the farmyard and turned left. I wanted to see Ellen for myself. I didn't believe Michael, when he said they couldn't find her. Ellen was strong and sensible. She was my friend and she had helped me and I hadn't been kind. I determined to call on her and put this right.

I walked along the track behind the farmhouse. I smiled to myself as I thought of the sight waiting for me round the bend. Maybe Ellen was also up early, and the oil lamp would be lit in the window of the cottage, just like when I stayed there. The mist will probably hang over the garden and make it look fairy-like, just like it did when I walked towards it on Christmas Eve. I turned the corner in the track, looked ahead of me and stopped dead. After a moment's pause to get over my shock, I walked slowly towards Ellen's cottage. Only it wasn't Ellen's cottage. It wasn't anyone's cottage. The cottage I was approaching was old, derelict and empty. The roof was gone, the door hung limply on rusted hinges, the garden was overgrown. I forced my way through the rusted gate, and the black empty windows stared at me as I struggled up the path. No-one had lived here for years and years and years.

Inside the door, the stairs and the first floor were still there, lying open to the stars. I climbed cautiously upwards, mindful of the old and rotten wood under my feet, and stared out across the garden and into the trees. This was what Michael wanted to keep me from, when he told me not to come. But where was Ellen? Who was Ellen?

Now I could only stand and wonder about what had happened to me since I'd come to stay at the farm, about the friendship Ellen had given me, which had made me feel less alone. And now I was alone after all; no Jacob, no Ellen, just me. But at the same time, no. I allowed myself the split-second memory of Jacob holding my hands in his, in Ellen's kitchen, and I knew I definitely wasn't alone. I breathed a deep sigh, leaned up against the empty window frame and looked across the trees for one last time.

Just then, I caught sight of a woman in a long black dress, disappearing through the trees into the mist...............................

Protect and Serve

There was something wrong with Bob.

His friend, Pete, came to this conclusion as he sat in their room in the White Hart Hotel and watched Bob as he slept. They'd been here for a week now, and whatever it was that was wrong with Bob had begun after they had arrived. Pete cast his mind back over the events of the last few days. They had arrived in the Forest of Dean and booked in at the White Hart, just like they had done for the previous four years. They came for a two-week contract, arranged with the Forestry people. Too many deer. They ruined everything. People like Pete and Bob dealt with them. Deer cullers. Acceptable killing.

But things were different when they'd arrived this time. The White Hart had changed hands. There was no friendly Mr and Mrs Jackson - Jimmy and Sue - to greet them. They'd sold up and moved on, and it had seemed to Pete and Bob that they'd deliberately sold their welcoming, friendly business to the weirdest and unfriendliest couple they could find. So - no greetings and cups of coffee when they'd arrived this time, no chats about what had been happening since last year's visit, just an air of suspicion and a grunt about how they'll "not find any deer round here. They keep themselves to themselves."

Pete and Bob had laughed about the strange 'local people' when they got up to their room, but what was stranger still, when they'd looked out of their bedroom window that evening, as the sun set, had been seeing their landlord feeding a couple of deer over the back fence. The deer seemed friendly - almost tame - as if he fed them like this every night.

And then there was the accident on the way into the forest. As Pete drove his 4x4 round a blind bend on the winding forest road, surrounded by nothing but trees, he'd almost crashed into a parked car. When they'd got out to investigate, he and Bob had found a young 'boy racer' type, angrily dragging the body of a huge stag off the road and into the roadside ditch.

"Bloody thing. Ran straight out in front of me. Look at my car!"
"Hmmm," Bob agreed as he bent down to inspect the crushed headlight and wing.
"We can tow you if you like," offered Pete.
"Stuff that," the young man had snorted. "It'll go alright."
"Ok, but what about the stag? You just leaving it there?"

"Yeah. You have it, if you're bothered so much."

The young man had revved up his car engine so that it scared everything within earshot, and raced off into the distance. Bob had looked at Pete.

"Shouldn't we report it?"

"Suppose so," said Pete. "We can ring when we get to the hotel."

There had been nothing unusual about some young kid hitting a deer on a quiet road. What was unusual was the headline in the local paper two days later.

"Here, Pete, look," Bob had said over breakfast. "Isn't that the boy we bumped into the other day?"

Bob had shown Pete the front-page headline:

YOUNG MAN KILLED IN UNEXPLAINED ROAD ACCIDENT AT NOTORIOUS 'DEER POOL' BLACK SPOT

A photograph of the same smiling young man in a cap accompanied the article.

"Yeah, that's him."

Pete had skimmed the article.

"Seems that there's a lot of accidents on this same bit of road."

"Not surprised, the way some of them drive," Bob had replied.

"Wonder what this 'Deer Pool' is?" Pete had asked. "I'll ask 'Happy Harry' on the way out."

"Why?"

"Because maybe there'll be plenty of deer there, stupid. Hence it's name."

They had encountered one crucial problem in this year's culling contract; they hadn't found any deer yet. Night after night they'd sat in their usual spots, deep in the trees, hidden in the bracken, signalling to each other, and hadn't seen a single deer. It was almost as if the deer had been warned to watch out.

"OK, Pete, we'll go to Deer Pool tonight."

Pete thought back to those words. Bob's last cheerful comment. Since then, he'd changed. He was moody and restless, pacing and impatient, trapped and withdrawn. It was something to do with the Deer Pool. That's what Pete had increasingly decided in his own mind. Things had changed after the night when Bob had fallen into the pool. He thought back to that night. It had been a starless night, black as pitch. The landlord of the White Hart had shown them where the pool was on a map. Pete remembered that he'd seemed reluctant to help, and that he and Bob had taken that as a good sign that they'd find deer there and finally earn some money.

They'd parked some way off, got out their rifles and walked carefully through the forest paths. Torches were obviously out, or everything within miles would see them coming. They knew they'd found the Deer Pool when they came across a blackness that looked different to the rest of the night.

The surface of the water seemed to shine a smooth black, reflected in a moon that wasn't there. It created a weird and sinister atmosphere. Anyway, both being hard, practical men and not given to creepy thoughts, they'd scouted about, found a couple of places to hide where they were about one hundred yards apart, and waited in the silence. This is what they always did; watched and waited for a sighting of a deer, then it was Pete's job to scare the deer and chase it, guiding it towards Bob, who'd pick it off with a single shot.

Bob had squatted down in the undergrowth. The Deer Pool was on his right, at the bottom of a grassy bank that sloped away from the path. His eyes had become accustomed to the darkness, and he could make out the shape of Pete's similarly squatted body beside a tree. He had just looked down to check that the catch was off on his gun, when suddenly there'd been a commotion. Bob had looked up just in time to see a huge stag racing towards him. No warning. No time to lose. Bob had jumped up, aimed at the stag, fired and missed. The stag had carried on towards him, its head down, antlers poised, and Bob knew his only chance was to jump out of the way. He'd jumped to the right, the ground fell away from him, and he'd rolled down, down, down, landing with a splash in filthy, stagnant Deer Pool. He'd disappeared under the water, then quickly appeared again, his thrashing, frightened movements making ripples across the pool's black surface. He'd felt his feet touch the bottom, since the pool wasn't very deep, and he'd struggled to climb out of the pool as he slipped about on the smooth rocks and slimy tree branches that littered the pool floor.

Fearing that Bob had drowned, Pete had run, jumped and slid to get to the water's edge. He'd grabbed his friend and pulled him onto the bank. Bob panted, out of breath from the fall and the shock.

"Jesus Christ, Pete, you could've given me a bit of notice."

"What're you talking about? I didn't send that stag. It just appeared from nowhere. It looked like it was going to charge you."

"I think it was. Only way I didn't get gouged was to fall in there. Oh, it stinks. Jesus! Jesus Christ and bloody hell!"

"Come on. We'll get back to the hotel and get you in a hot shower." That had been three days ago, and Bob had never been the same since.

*   *   *

Just then Bob stirred. He opened his eyes, woke up properly and noticed Pete sitting at the end of the bed.

"Hey, Pete. What's up?"

"Nothing. Just waiting for you to wake up. You've been out for hours."

Bob looked at the alarm clock on the bedside table.

"Eleven! I didn't think I'd slept that long!"

"Must've needed it," Pete replied.

"I had a horrible dream. And I've got a stinking headache. Right across here."

Bob waved his hand across his forehead, to indicate where his head hurt.

"I'll find you a coffee and some paracetamol. What did you dream about?"

"I dreamt I was running through the woods. Fast, like I was being chased. And I was scared. Really scared. I was scared I wouldn't get away. Anyway, coffee'd be good. I'm going to have a quick shower and..........."

As he spoke, Bob threw the quilt back so he could get up. He froze, staring. Pete stared too. Bob lay in his bed, completely naked, covered in mud. Dark, thick mud. Forest mud. He looked at Pete.

"I thought I was dreaming."

Pete couldn't think of anything to say.

"Did I go out last night? Pete? Did I go out?"

"Dunno. I slept like a log."

Downstairs in the bar, Pete rang the bell on the counter. The landlady appeared.

"Morning. I'm sorry to bother you. I wondered if you had a couple of paracetamol for my friend?"

The landlady looked at Pete. Without replying, she disappeared into the door marked 'Private' and came back with a packet of aspirin.

"That's all I have," she muttered.

"Thanks. That's great."

Pete stopped as he turned to go back upstairs. He looked at the landlady. She stared back.

"Bob - my friend - he fell into the Deer Pool, three nights ago. He's not really been right since. Do you know if there's anything wrong with the water? You know, like an algae, or a bacteria? Sometimes you get warned about these things, don't you, in the paper and........................"

Pete's voice trailed off when he realised he wasn't generating any response from the landlady. She just seemed bored.

"Well, never mind. Thanks for the tablets."

He walked towards the stairs.

"The Deer Pool is a very old pool," the landlady called after him. "Goes back a long time."

Pete smiled politely as he started up the stairs.

"Thanks for that."

Back upstairs, Bob had showered and dressed. He looked much brighter as he sat on his bed, leaning up against the headrest.

"How you feeling?"

"Bit better. My head still hurts, though."

Pete filled the glass that sat by the sink with water and handed it to Bob, along with the tablets.

"Thanks. You know, I still feel tired. Isn't that weird, after all that sleep?"

"Maybe you need some fresh air. We could go for a stroll, out the back there. Not go far."

"OK. I don't know what the landlady will say about my sheets. They're covered in mud. I don't understand that."

"Nor me. Maybe you went sleepwalking."

Bob laughed.

"With no clothes on!"

"It's been known to happen. She'll just not have to mind. There's not much she can do about it, is there? Anyway, you pull yourself together. I'll meet you in the bar. I'm going for a pint."

Half an hour later, Pete and Bob set off through the back gate of the hotel. By now the hot sun was high above them, and they were glad of the protection which the trees gave them as they strolled along. They walked in single file, Bob staying a few yards ahead of Pete.

"I was thinking, Bob, if you're still not feeling well by the end of the week, we may as well call it a day here and just cancel the job. We've had sod all luck so far."

"I know, but we need to earn something, cover our costs at least. Why d'you think we're having so much trouble this year? There were loads of deer last year, and the year before."

"If you're up to it, we'll try again tonight. What do you think?"

Bob didn't answer. Pete noticed that Bob had stopped walking, and Pete quickly caught him up. Bob was staring into the trees. Pete looked at him. Bob seemed strange, head up, listening and alert.

"What's up?"

"There's a funny smell. I'm trying to work out what it is."

"I can't smell anything."

"Wait." Bob turned to Pete. "It's you. I can smell you."

"Hey, steady on a minute. What are you talking about?"

Pete's legs suddenly went shaky as he watched Bob's face transform, caught by a look of uncontrollable terror.

"You!" Bob shouted. "I can smell you and you're after me!"

Pete looked around, uncomfortable. He laughed nervously.

"Stop it, Bob. You're being weird."

"No, I'm not. Get away! Get away from me!"

Suddenly Bob shot off into the trees. He crashed randomly along, leaving the path behind, as he ran in a blind panic. Pete chased after him.

"Bob! Wait! What's the hell's wrong with you?"

Bob ran on, ducking and weaving. Pete lost sight of him but carried on regardless. Finally, Pete arrived in a clearing. In front of him stood a derelict building, an old stone cottage with broken walls and no roof. Pete stopped to study it. There was no sign of Bob. Slowly and cautiously, just like when he went hunting, Pete circled the building, looking for a way to see inside. As he turned the corner, he found a gap in the wall, and there was Bob, crouched low against the inside of the wall, watching him. He seemed calmer, and stayed still as Pete approached him.

"Ssssh! Bob, are you OK?"

Bob looked at Pete, met his gaze, and Pete was relieved to see recognition in Bob's eyes. He walked slowly up to Bob and crouched down next to him. Bob turned to him. Pete laughed gently.

"Hey, you gave me a fright there. What's wrong?"

Bob looked directly at Pete.

"I was here last night, Pete. I knew this building was here, because I hid in it last night."

Pete looked at Bob, then stood up.

"Right, we're going back to the hotel. Come on."

"Why?"

"Because we're packing up and going home," Pete replied, hoping that the assertiveness in his voice would work.

Bob got up.

"My headache is worse," was all he said, and then they walked back in silence.

Back at the hotel, Bob looked positively ill. As he and Pete walked into the bar, everyone - the landlord and landlady, the customers - stopped talking and watched his progress towards the stairs.

"You go on upstairs, Bob. I'll tell the landlord our plans."

Pete watched Bob as he slowly began to climb the stairs.

"You look terrible. You need to lie down and get some rest."

Pete turned. It was the landlady who had spoken, and he was caught completely off guard by her sudden concern and interest.

"Yes. Bob's headache is worse. He's going to lie down."

"He fell in the Deer Pool," said the landlady out loud, as if to the whole room. A ripple of murmurs and mutterings passed across the bar, as if everyone now understood the nature of Bob's condition.

"I've got to lie down," Bob whispered.

"OK. I'll be up in a second."

Pete walked over to the bar, aware that everyone seemed to be watching him. He could hear a loud clock ticking somewhere. At the counter, the landlord smiled. Pete realised that he'd never seen him smile yet, and that the smile sat wrongly on the man's face, making him seem sinister and malicious.

"We've decided not to stay until the end of the week," he said to the smiling face. "Bob seems to be getting worse and we're going to go home.

So, if you can settle our bill after tonight, we'll pay in the morning."

"Shouldn't you wait and see how your friend is in the morning?"

"Perhaps, but that's our plan as things stand at the moment."

"Your friend needs rest. Lots of rest."

Pete turned to see who spoke. It was the old man in the corner. He usually sat there in the afternoons, and played crib or dominoes with a couple of other guests.

"He's got a long journey ahead of him," the old man continued.

"What do you mean?"

"Oh, don't mind him," interrupted the landlady. "He rambles on. He means you've got a long drive tomorrow, that's all."

"Yes," the old man said. "My old mother used to say that sleep fixed everything."

Pete smiled politely at him as he walked past and headed for the stairs. Everyone watched him go up the stairs and disappear out of sight.

"Trouble is, sleeping won't do a bit of damn good, with what that fellow's got."

The old man smiled knowingly, looking at everyone else in the bar.

Upstairs, Bob was already tucked up in bed, fast asleep. Pete watched him. He was confused by all this weird business. It was new to him and challenged his view of the world. He knew he didn't know what to do, other than take Bob home, get him away from this environment and see if that helped him get back to normal. As for himself, Pete decided he would have a shower and drive into town for the evening. He wanted to find some other company that was less claustrophobic, to while away his last evening. As the sun began to set, Bob was still sleeping soundly. He seemed fine and his breathing was regular and calm. Pete left Bob a note by his bed to explain where he'd gone, and crept quietly out of the room.

After a couple of pints, a decent bar meal and a game of pool with friendly strangers, Pete headed back to the hotel at about eleven o'clock. He nodded to the landlord as he walked through the bar and went straight upstairs. He opened the door to his room slowly and quietly and walked in, expecting Bob to be asleep. In the dark, the hairs on the back of his neck stood up as he saw the moonlight shining through the open window, the curtains billowing in a night breeze, and Bob - Bob climbing carefully back in the window, naked and covered in mud. Halfway into the window, Bob stopped and stared at Pete. Pete stared back.

"It's late," Pete said, cautiously. Bob smiled a strange smile.

"I know," he said.

"Do you want a hand?" Pete continued.

"No, I'm alright. I think I did this last night as well."

Pete watched Bob as he navigated the edge of the window frame and then stood in the room, looking round. Something was wrong with him. In the darkness, his head seemed just a touch misshapen.

"Where've you been, Bob? Why did you go out the window? And with no clothes on?"

Bob seemed uncertain. Pete stepped closer to him, but Bob backed away a little.

"Have you been fighting?" Pete challenged. Bob's forehead was noticeably swollen, different to when he'd gone to bed earlier. It was grazed, red and bleeding from a deep cut above each eye.

"I'm tired," was all Bob said.

He made a move towards his bed, and Pete sprang across the room. He grabbed Bob and whispered into his ear.

"No, Bob. You can't go to sleep. Not yet. I want you to tell me where you've been."

Bob struggled, but Pete held him firm. They bumped the chest-of-drawers, causing a loud clashing sound as it banged against the wall.

"Stop it, Bob. Keep still and be quiet. The last thing we need is those weirdos downstairs coming up and seeing you in that state!"

Bob relaxed and he and Pete sank down onto the bed. Pete let Bob go and watched him. Bob seemed different; alive, his eyes bright.

"I was fighting with a stag," he whispered.

"What! What the hell are you talking about?"

"You know, like stags fight - head to head. I had hold of its antlers, like this.........." Bob held imaginary antlers in the air, to illustrate what he meant, "and we rolled and fell, banging our heads together."

Pete thought before he spoke.

"What did you do that for?"

Pete didn't know what to say or what to do. He couldn't believe his ears.

"I don't know why. It just felt right."

Suddenly Bob's eyes began to close. Pete jumped up.

"No, Bob. Don't go to sleep. Please. I think we need to get you to a doctor. Right now."

"Please, Pete." Bob spoke in that lazy, slurry tone people have when they just can't stay awake. "Let me go to sleep. We can talk about it tomorrow."

Bob lay down on the bed as he spoke, and instantly fell into a deep sleep. Pete was frightened and concerned by now, but he didn't have the heart to disturb his friend. He covered Bob's naked, muddy body with a quilt, and went downstairs to the bar.

In the bar, Pete bought a pint of beer and sat in the corner. He didn't want to talk to anyone. He just watched. Did the landlord know what was going on? Should he confide in him, or would that be a mistake? Pete knew that he was being watched in return.

Every time his eyes left part of the bar and then went back again, people averted their own eyes. What was the matter? What was going on? Eventually Pete finished his drink and went upstairs. This time, when he opened the bedroom door, Bob was fast asleep where he'd left him. Pete closed the window and the curtains, and went to bed as well. Home in the morning. That's for sure.

Pete woke in the morning to the sound of screaming. At first he was confused, then he realised it was Bob who was screaming; high, pitiful, painful cries. Pete woke up properly with a start and jumped out of bed. Bob was sitting up in bed, cradling his head in his hands.

"Do something! I can't stand this! Help me! Someone help me!"

Bob lifted his head and Pete took a step back, shocked at Bob's appearance. His head was swollen above his eyes. His forehead was rounded and pronounced, and the swelling forced his eyelids down and to the sides. Above each eye, set in the general swelling, lay two definite round bumps, forcing their way out, tearing at Bob's skin.

"Jesus, Bob. What's going on? We've got to get you to a hospital. Right now!"

Bob lay down.

"I can't go anywhere. It hurts too much."

He scrabbled around on the bedside table and found the aspirin. He gulped a handful down with some water, then lay back, in obvious agony.

"I can't move off this bed."

"Then I'm going for a doctor. I'll get the landlord to come up and sit with you."

Pete looked at Bob again for a split second, then he shot out of the room. Downstairs, he ran across the bar to the counter. The landlady was putting glasses away, and she turned round to look at him.

"Bob," he gasped in panic, "He's really ill. I'm going to find a doctor. Can you look after him?"

Pete raced off without waiting for a reply and the landlady watched as his 4x4 sped off down the drive. Slowly and calmly, she finished what she was doing and then went upstairs. She walked in without knocking and found Bob curled up on the bed. She sat down beside him.

"Sit up," she said sharply. "Let me have a look at you."

Bob did as the landlady requested. He sat back against the headrest as she looked with interest at his swollen head. She reached out to touch the two bumps above his eyes, and he flinched, trying to deflect her touch. She seemed interested in Bob's head, and unconcerned about him. Bob watched her. Suddenly she spoke, gently and soothingly.

"Yes, I see what's happening."

"What? What is it?"

"You see, you should have left the deer alone. People like you, think you know it all. We warned you, and you went after them."

"Please - I don't understand."

"You will. Soon."

Tears sprang into Bob's eyes. He stared at the landlady. She stared back at his sad, scared face, the grotesque swelling making him seem all the more pathetic.

"Please help me. It hurts."

The landlady stood up.

"I'll be back in a little while."

Bob cried now. Tears rolled down his cheeks.

"But that's no good. Please do something now."

He looked at her and whispered 'please' again. She walked out of the room, and Bob lay down, cradling his head in his hands.

Just then, Pete pulled up outside. He was alone. He ran in.

"What kind of place is this? There's not a doctor anywhere can come."

The landlady shrugged.

"That's how things are done round here."

Above them, muffled sounds came from the direction of Bob's room. It sounded like someone was struggling or falling about.

"Bob................."

Pete's voice trailed off and then suddenly, a single gunshot broke the silence. Pete raced up the stairs two at a time. He burst through the bedroom door, and then swayed in the doorway, legs unsteady, as he saw Bob lying across the bed, saw his rifle next to him, saw the gaping hole where his forehead should have been, the darkness seeping onto the floor. Pete saw all this, and he cried.

*　　　*　　　*

Blue lights flashed in the background. Pete sat on the hotel steps, staring straight ahead into the trees. He knew they had put Bob in the ambulance; zipped him up in a bag and laid him out. He knew their bedroom was taped off with tape saying 'Police Crime Scene'. He knew that Bob had shot himself. Pete knew all of these things, but he didn't know why. He continued to stare while, out of the corner of his eye, he saw the detective stroll towards him.

"Mr Shepherd. Can I ask you a few questions?"

Pete looked at the detective now.

"Did you know that Mr Johnson was unstable?"

"He wasn't unstable."

"Well, he's just made a nice mess of his hotel room, proving it."

Pete was angry.

"Something happened to him."

The detective paused, making notes.

"When?"

"After he fell in the Deer Pool."

"Ah! Yes. The Deer Pool. So, what do you think happened to him?"

"I don't know. Just, he was never the same after he fell in. I don't know what it means."

The detective put his notebook away.

"Well, they're taking his body to the local chapel of rest. I understand it's all arranged for one of my men to drive your car back to town. You being in shock and all."

Pete didn't reply.

"We've got your address and phone details, so we'll be in touch, about the inquest and so on. And when you know what's happening about funerals and such, just give us a call."

Pete watched the detective as he walked off.

"Don't you care? About my friend?"

The detective looked back at him

"Just doing my job."

Pete felt hot tears prick his eyes. Something had happened to his friend. Something had happened, and nobody cared.

Half an hour later, Pete's 4x4 rolled out of the drive, driven by a local policeman. Pete watched the hotel disappear from view, then he stared in silence out of the car window.

Back at the hotel, the landlord stood at the back fence. He clicked his tongue, then he looked into the trees, as if expecting something. After a few minutes, a herd of deer emerged from the trees. The landlord watched as the deer approached the fence. Then, lovingly, they pushed their heads up and over the fence, allowing him to stroke them. All the time, he talked soothingly and quietly to the deer.

Behind him, the landlady appeared.

"Look," she whispered, almost in reverence.

The landlord looked in the direction she indicated, and saw a single young stag walking along the fence line towards them. The other deer watched the stag approach. The landlord smiled.

"It's alright. He's come to join you," he said.

There was an expectant pause while the deer collectively seemed to consider the stag, and then suddenly they all darted off into the woods, taking the new stag with them. The landlord smiled and watched them go. He put his arm round his wife and they set off back up the garden. As they walked, they both glanced up at the window of the room where Bob and Pete had stayed, and where Bob had died. They smiled a knowing smile to each other, and disappeared inside the hotel.

The Naming of Trees

Harry rushed around the kitchen, trying to fasten his tie and make a cup of coffee at the same time. He was never organized in the mornings, not since Libby had gone, and every morning he told himself this. He had told himself this for the last fifteen months, and nothing had changed. Finally Harry ate a tasteless piece of toast, finished his coffee and grabbed his briefcase. As he walked towards the front door, the letterbox opened and a pile of post dropped onto the mat. He was in a hurry. He was always late. Should he step over the post, go to work and look at it on the way back in tonight, or should he stop now and see what's there?

When Harry reached the door, the decision was made for him. He saw the corner of a postcard sticking out from in between the collection of envelopes and junk mail. He picked up all the post, but only the postcard interested him. On the front of the postcard he saw a photograph of a forest scene, extending away into the distance. In the foreground lay an atmospheric pond with mist hanging on the top of it. A message printed at the top of the postcard said 'Greetings From the Forest of Dean'.

"So," Harry said out loud. "Back in England, eh?"
He turned the postcard over and read the message. It was the same as always:

"Hello, Harry. Hope you're well, Libby."

Harry sighed; for a second he had allowed himself to hope for more this time. He went into his study. A collection of postcards was pinned to a cork notice board on the wall next to his desk. He pinned the 'Forest of Dean' card up there with the others, then stood back, as he had done many times during the last fifteen months, to study them all. The collection of postcards contained a variety of images from all parts of Europe; golden beaches, wide lakes, high mountains, cows with bells on, snowy peaks in winter, fairy castles, busy streets and ancient monuments. Yes, Libby had managed to travel far. Harry knew that much. It was the how and why that bothered him. But never mind - she was home at last. Or at least, back in England. Harry tapped the Forest of Dean postcard, as if doing this confirmed this knowledge to him, and then he picked up his briefcase again and left for work.

*   *   *

Libby was hot. She lay in the back of the van and tried to read, while Jim negotiated the twists and turns of the famous winding Forest of Dean roads. Eventually Libby gave up trying to read and tapped on the window that separated the living area of the van from the driver's compartment. Jim turned his head briefly towards her and grinned. He pulled into the side of the road and waited while Libby got out of the van and climbed up next to him.

"I can't read with all this jostling about," she moaned.

"Sorry," Jim replied. "Still, we're nearly there now."

They drove on. Libby admired the view. She'd never been to the Forest of Dean before, whereas Jim, in his own words, was a 'veteran visitor'. He glanced at Libby as he drove.

"Did you send your postcard?"

"I did, when we stopped in Newnham."

Jim paused before he answered.

"That's good. Really good."

They drove on in silence now. Eventually, they came upon a hand-painted sign that said 'Severn Revels - Performer's Campsite. Next left into field.'

"Here we are. That's us," said Jim, and he swung the van left through a gate and into a huge field. A few tents and vans like Jim's were parked around the edge, but it was generally still quite empty. Jim chose a spot and parked up.

"I'm going to have a look around, see who else is here," Libby said as she jumped out of the van.

Jim waved a 'carry on' at her, then he went round to the back of the van, found a bottle of beer in the van's refrigerator, and sat down to relax after his long drive.

*　　　*　　　*

Six hours after receiving Libby's latest postcard, Harry was speeding down the motorway, not caring if he ramped the car or not. It wasn't his; company car, company petrol. He smiled to himself as he thought back to that morning, how he'd gone to work and persuaded his line manager, Mike, to give him a week's leave on the spot. Mike was good to Harry. He was a company line manager who had managed to stay a little bit human. He was the only person at work who knew about Libby, and so he also knew how important it was for Harry to get to the Forest of Dean there and then. Mike knew how much Harry needed to find his wife. Harry drove without a break, even though he knew he shouldn't, and he passed a sign saying 'Welcome to the Forest of Dean' at about six-thirty in the evening. He followed the directions that had been given to him on the phone, headed for Coleford, and soon found the B'n'B he'd booked. He parked outside, rang the front door bell, and an old lady answered.

"Mrs Matthews?" he asked.

"Yes. You must be Mr Johnson. Come on in."

Harry followed Mrs Matthews into the hallway, where she gave him the guest book to fill in. Harry was aware that as he wrote in the book, she watched him carefully. He found this both amusing and a little unsettling.

"Old forest folk," he laughed to himself, as he followed Mrs Matthews to his room.

"It's very nice. Thank you."

"Here's a key for the front door, and this one is your room key. Breakfast is between eight and ten. You're also welcome to use the lounge downstairs if you want to watch television while you're here."

"Thank you," Harry said again.

"Oh - apart from tonight. Tonight I have a meeting in there, so it's not available. I have a meeting every Tuesday and Thursday, at seven o'clock on the dot."

"OK," said Harry, wondering if he was supposed to show an interest in the 'meeting'.

"Well, just give me a shout if you want anything."

Harry smiled and watched Mrs Matthews as she disappeared down the hallway.

"Local people," he laughed to himself.

Harry decided to relax for the rest of the evening. He would start looking for Libby tomorrow. He showered and changed, then went for a walk around the town. After a decent bar meal and a couple of pints in a local pub, he strolled back to the B'n'B at about nine o'clock. As Harry let himself in, the door of the lounge opened abruptly. Mrs Matthews and another elderly lady came out. They both stared at Harry. Harry stared back. The elderly lady spoke first.

"Is this him?"

"Yes," said Mrs Matthews.

"What?" said Harry.

"Please, come and join us," the elderly lady continued. "We have some information for you." Harry's head suddenly spun. Information? It must be about Libby. He quickly composed himself again - got to stay in control.

"Please," Mrs Matthews said gently, interrupting Harry's train of thought. "Come in." Harry followed the two women into the lounge. Once inside, he saw a group of six or seven people, drinking tea and coffee and eating biscuits. They all looked at him at once as he entered the room, and Harry found himself trying not to laugh, because they seemed such an odd bunch.

"You just missed our meeting. Would you like a cup of tea?"

Mrs Matthews had appeared at Harry's side, and waited for an answer. Harry looked at her.

"No, thank you. Er - so what's the information you have for me?"

Mrs Matthews smiled.

"Sit down," she said.

Harry sat down, trying his best to feel comfortable with a group of people he never expected to meet. A man about Harry's age leaned forward.

"Hello. I'm Jack. It's me who got the message for you."

Harry just stared at Jack, not sure what he was supposed to say. Jack looked around at the others.

"He doesn't know what we do," he said.

"Ah!" said Mrs Matthews, as if struck by a moment of clarity. She turned to Harry.

"We're spiritualists," she said. "We hold our weekly meetings here."

Harry began to feel uncomfortable. This was completely unfamiliar territory for him. Also, he reasoned, does this mean that the 'message' they have will tell him that Libby is dead? He noticed his heart rate go faster and he felt a little bit sick. Jack spoke again.

"I had a message, loud and clear. 'Tell Harry that he will find everything he needs, here in the forest.' That was the message."

Harry wasn't going to tell these people his business. He simply shrugged his shoulders.

"Doesn't mean anything to me, I'm afraid. With this sort of.........stuff, do you get to know who the message came from?"

Jack looked at Harry before he answered. Harry really felt as if all this was invading his personal space.

"Yes. The message was from Luke."

Harry froze. He found the strength to remain outwardly calm, but inside, he felt his stomach churn, his knees turn to jelly, his head start to spin. He quickly composed himself again, hoping no-one had noticed.

"I'm really sorry, it really doesn't mean anything to me," he said, shaking his head.

"Really? He said the message was for Harry."

The group seemed disappointed. Harry continued his apologetic act as he stood up to leave.

"I have to go. I'm really sorry if I seem ungrateful or unhelpful. Thank you. Goodnight."

The group remained seated and watched Harry as he hurried out of the lounge. Once he had closed the lounge door, he quietly left the house again instead of going to his room. Out in the street, he walked through town until he found an off-licence that was still open. He bought a large bottle of Jack Daniels, took it back to his room and drank it all.

*   *   *

At the campsite, Libby bounced jubilantly across the grass towards Jim. He was sitting outside the van with his third bottle of beer, and he laughed at Libby as she approached.

"Jill's here, and Steve and Sarah, and Pete's on his way."

"Great," Jim said. "See - I told you they'd find it alright."

"I know, I know. Jill said they're all just settling in, then there'll be beers, music and a bonfire."

"You're like a kid, d'you know? Anyway, don't drink a lot tonight,

because I've got something to show you in the morning. A surprise."
Libby jumped down beside him.

"What is it? Tell me, Jim."

"No. It's a surprise. I said that already."

"I'm going back over to Jill. Can I take a couple of beers?"

"Help yourself. I'll be over in a bit."

Jim watched Libby as she raced back across the field. He grinned. It was good to see her feeling so positive. Jim lay down in the sun and closed his eyes. He wasn't in any hurry to start socializing after the long drive. Jill wouldn't mind. They'd travelled together for years. This was all new to Libby. Let her enjoy the space.

Later that evening, as the sun began to set and the twilight world took over, Jim strolled towards the huge bonfire that had been built near the centre of the field. Lots more people had arrived now. There were tents and vans everywhere, and people sat in groups playing musical instruments or chatting together. As Jim got close to the bonfire, he stopped to watch a couple of people who were practicing their juggling act. First they used clubs, then they changed to burning torches. The light of the flames made weird circles in the darkness as they flew round and round above their heads. Jim clapped and they gave him mock bows. He walked on and found Libby, Sarah and Jill trying some improvised folk dancing, while Pete and Steve played a duet on a fiddle and a guitar. The girls stopped dancing and ran to hug Jim. Pete and Steve winked in Jim's direction as they continued to play. Jim whispered in Sarah's ear.

"I told her not to drink too much."

Sarah play-punched Jim's arm.

"Oh, leave her alone. She's fine. She's doing well."

Jim laughed as he cracked open another bottle of beer, while Sarah gave him a look that said "You're a fine one to talk".

The rest of the evening was hazy for everyone. The beer flowed free, the music was loud and frantic, the bonfire burned. The atmosphere of the campsite was happy and content as people danced, talked, kissed and cuddled into the early hours.

Next morning, Libby paid a heavy price.

"I have a bad head!" she moaned, when Jim shook her awake in her bed in the back of the van. It was six o'clock.

"OK. I'll give you half an hour, then it's out of bed and a cup of black coffee, otherwise I'm going on my own."

"Thank you, Jim," Libby mumbled, asleep before she'd finished speaking. Half an hour later, Libby was sitting up in bed drinking the required black coffee. She made a face. Jim laughed.

"Not funny."

"I know. Sorry, but come on. Hurry up. I want to show you

something that you'll only catch this early."

Jim waited outside the van until Libby eventually appeared, looking grim.

"Right, then. We have to walk. This way."

Libby followed Jim as they headed out of the campsite via a stile in the fence and set off into the woods. They walked deep into the trees, following a well-trodden path as it climbed up and over a hill and down into a dip. Finally they came across a pond set in the middle of the trees, quite remote, nothing nearby. Jim watched Libby's face as she stared at the view before her. The early morning mist hung a couple of feet above the surface of the water, which was completely still. Not a ripple in sight. The trees stretched away in every direction. The picture that was created was one of total calm and peace.

"Oh, Jim. It's beautiful!" Libby whispered, almost in reverence.

"This is why you had to get up early. You'd miss the mist otherwise."

"And the trees," Libby continued. "Just look at all the trees. I've got plenty to choose from here."

Jim sat down on the horizontal trunk of a tree that had probably blown over in the wind, and watched Libby. First of all she stood for a moment taking in the view, then she began to walk slowly round the edge of the pond. She walked up to one of the trees - a tall, slim larch - and carefully reached out to touch its rough bark. She turned briefly to smile at Jim, then she walked further into the trees. Yes, Jim mused, he was right to bring Libby here. It was just what she needed. He continued to watch her as she strolled away from him, then he got out his tobacco and papers. He lit his roll-up and blew out a puff of smoke that mingled with the early morning air. He'd wait here for Libby, just like always.

Minutes later, the silence of the moment was broken by a scream. He sat up like a shot and listened. A second scream, and then another. It was Libby.

"Libby? Libby!" he shouted out loud, as he jumped up in a panic and ran towards the sound. He crashed through the ferns and bracken, looking in all directions, and then finally saw Libby. She was curled up on the ground, leaning against a tree, with her knees pulled up close. She was in obvious distress.

"Libby! What's wrong? Are you hurt?"

Jim examined her quickly but could see no signs of any injury. He looked around but the forest was empty.

"It was a boy, Jim. A little boy."

Libby threw herself into Jim's arms and sobbed. Jim was unsure about what to do. He held onto Libby while she cried and looked around.

"What do you mean, Libby? What little boy?"

Jim held Libby at arms length now and looked her in the eye.

"Over there. I looked over there and he was watching me, from behind that tree."

She continued to cry. Jim let go of Libby, sat her carefully down and went to investigate. He wandered about in the trees, looking in all directions, but there was no-one in sight. He walked back to Libby.

"I can't see anyone."

"I definitely saw him."

"OK. What did he look like?"

"Oh, he was only little, about two years old." Libby smiled a little at the memory. "He had dark hair and he was wearing a blue coat and jeans, and wellies. You know, those kiddies' wellies with frogs on."

"There's no-one here. Look, he was probably out for an early morning walk with his parents and wandered off from them. When you screamed, he probably ran back to them. Bet you gave him a fright, eh?"

Jim was trying to lighten the situation, because he didn't like this one bit.

"No, he wasn't with anyone. I'm sure he was all on his own."

"You can't be sure, Libby."

"But what scared me was that he was watching me, like he'd been watching me for a while before I noticed him. And it was the way he was looking at me. He had these eyes...."

Libby started to cry again.

"Come on, we're going back to the van."

They walked back in silence. Jim kept his arm round Libby all the way. She didn't speak. Back at the van, Jim made Libby go back to bed and then he sat with her until she fell asleep. Some rest will be the best thing, he decided. Libby slept until lunchtime and woke up feeling much better. She joined Jim, who was sitting on the grass outside the van, enjoying the sun.

"Hey," he said simply when he saw her.

"Hey," she replied weakly.

"How're you feeling?"

"Alright. Sorry about earlier."

"No need to apologise. Gave me a fright, that's all."

"Jim - let's not tell anyone, OK?"

"OK. Fine by me. Look, it was just some kid out in the woods. You'll not see him again."

"Probably not."

"So, are you up for going into town this afternoon? We need to do some stuff - hand out leaflets."

"Sure. That'd be great. I'm going to see Jill for a minute."

"Cool," replied Jim, and watched Libby as she walked across the field, until she was right out of view.

*   *   *

Harry had also woken with a hangover. He discreetly hid the empty Jack Daniels bottle in his luggage, and then set off into town. The Tourist

Information Office supplied him with lists of accommodation, and he began his search. Campsites first. People with no money usually camp, he'd decided; during the last fifteen months, Harry had made sure there was always cash in their bank account in case Libby needed it, but she'd never used it. After the fruitless searches of seven different campsites, Harry felt despondent. He pulled in at a 'greasy spoon' roadside café in a quiet lay by, bought a coffee and settled himself into one of the café's white plastic chairs. He pondered over his situation. It was like looking for a needle in a haystack, trying to find Libby here on the basis of one postcard. Should he be looking at campsites? He tried to rationalize this, and couldn't. Well, he would continue to check the other campsites, one by one, until he'd visited them all, and then he'd try the guesthouses and hotels. He wouldn't give up. Couldn't give up. He'd look and look and look until he found Libby. His plan had to work.

But just then, Harry found Libby, by accident. He was sitting in a queue of traffic, passing through town, when he saw her. It took him a moment to be sure. She looked different. Her hair was dyed a strange red, she was dressed differently, in jeans and an old baggy T-shirt, but it was her. He was sure. She was standing outside one of the high street shops, handing out leaflets to people as they passed by. And she wasn't alone. A tall man, about Harry's age, stood next to her. He was also handing out leaflets. Harry pulled his car in on the side of the road and watched them. When they finished handing out their leaflets, Harry watched Libby and the man as they climbed into a battered old traveller van. He followed in his car as they drove off, left town and headed into open countryside. When the van eventually turned left into a field at a sign saying 'Severn Revels - Performers Campsite. Next left into field', Harry drove straight past. He parked on the side of the road a little further on, and set off back towards the campsite on foot. Instead of going in through the main entrance, he found a gap in the hedge and climbed through. He then proceeded to skirt the edge of the campsite, trying to avoid being seen, looking all the time for Libby.

He saw them. Libby and that man. They were in the middle of the field, in a space created when the various vans and tents had congregated around the edge. He watched the two of them as they messed about, trying out some acrobatic tricks. The man knelt down so that Libby could climb up onto his shoulders, and then he tried to stand up with her perched precariously above him. It wasn't generally working, and Libby and the man fell about laughing every time their attempts failed and they ended up in a heap on the ground. As Harry watched them from his hideout behind a nearby tent, he became filled with a mixture of emotions; anger, envy, fear, confusion. What should he do? What should he do? He continued to watch as the man knelt down again, Libby climbed up on his shoulders again, they fell over again. They laughed again. They were laughing together. It was obvious that they were having fun. Eventually they stopped their rehearsal and sat talking. Harry couldn't hear what they were saying, but then Libby stood up and walked off. He watched Libby disappear from view, and then he watched the man as he stood up and walked over to his van. Harry could contain himself no longer. He didn't care about hiding any more. He marched straight across the middle of the field.

He arrived at the van and found the man with his head deep underneath the bonnet, tinkering with something. He didn't notice Harry until the last moment. He stood up straight and managed to say "Can I help you?" before Harry swung his arm back and punched him full on the jaw. Caught unexpectedly, the man fell backwards onto the grass. He looked up at Harry, who lunged at him, caught hold of him by his collar, and hit him again.

"Who are you? Who are you?" Harry snarled quietly into Jim's face.

"I'm Jim. My name's Jim," Jim managed to say through the blood that was beginning to trickle from his mouth.

"I don't care what your name is. Who are you? What are you doing with Libby? Why are you here with her?"

Jim stared at Harry for a second.

"Oh, God. You're Harry," he said, then he jumped to his feet. Jim was ready for Harry now. The element of surprise was gone, but Harry was still enraged. He lunged at Jim, who simply stepped to one side. Harry tripped and fell, rolling on the ground at Jim's feet. He lay there, out of breath, staring at his opponent.

"Listen," said Jim. "You can hit me as many times as you like, but it won't do Libby any good."

Harry didn't speak. He didn't do anything. He just stared at Jim. Jim knew that Harry wasn't really a threat. He could tell that Harry wasn't really a fighter. He held his hand out to Harry.

"Here. Get up. We need to talk."

Harry refused Jim's extended hand and got up by himself. He dusted himself down, feeling a little foolish after his tussle, but not prepared to admit it. Jim went to the refrigerator and produced two bottles of beer.

"Want a drink?"

Harry nodded 'yes'.

"Here," Jim opened both bottles, passed one to Harry, then sat down on the grass. Harry watched Jim, then sat down at a short distance from him. Jim took a swig from his beer, aware that Harry was staring at him.

"What?" Jim finally asked.

"So, have you been sleeping with her?"

Harry didn't expect Jim to be so surprised at the question. He expected him to say 'yes'.

"I said, have you slept with her? With Libby?"

"Listen, mate. You've got it all wrong," was Jim's reply. Harry was angry again. The beer was giving him more confidence.

"Really?" he said, raising his voice. "What exactly is it I've got wrong? I finally trace my wife after fifteen months, to this backwoods of a place, and the first time I see her, she's with you. I follow you both here, and you're larking about on the grass, and sharing this dump of a van. So, what am I getting wrong?"

"For a start, there's nothing going on between me and Libby, and there never has been. She's travelled with me, or rather, with us. Our larger group of friends. She's over with a couple of them now. Look, I'll show you something."

Jim got up and went round to the back of the van. He opened the back doors and looked at Harry, inviting him to have a look. Harry did, and saw that the interior of the van had been converted into a tidy living area. There were two single beds built up against the two sides of the van, and at the front there was a small cupboard placed between them. At the rear of the van, just next to the back doors, a small sink had been installed next to a small stove and an equally small refrigerator. Everything was small. Compact. Harry looked at Jim.

"Did you do all this?"

"Yeah. Me and my brother did it. Neat, isn't it?"

"That's not what I'd call it."

Harry sounded sarcastic. Jim looked at Harry, weighed him up, and decided to give him the benefit of the doubt, since he didn't really know him. Maybe he's not an idiot. Maybe he's just acting like one.

"Anyway," Jim continued, "That's where Libby sleeps, and that's where I sleep, when we're both sleeping in here. Sometimes Libby sleeps over in someone else's van. Just depends. It's all very relaxed," Jim paused, then said, "and that's how it's been for the last fifteen months."

Harry seemed calmer.

"Look, mate. Me and your wife, we're just friends."

Jim realised that there were tears in Harry's eyes.

"I think I know how she got here," Harry whispered.

"OK."

The two men sat back down on the grass. Jim was quiet, and paid attention totally to Harry, without interrupting, as his tale unfolded.

"Luke was our first baby," Harry began. "He was lovely. He had these huge blue eyes and this gorgeous smile."

Harry stopped abruptly.

"What's wrong?" Jim asked quietly.

"I just realized, I never described him to anyone before."

Harry got up and walked off. He stopped a little way off and seemed to stare into space. Jim stayed quiet and watched. Presently, Harry came back and sat down again.

"That's it, really."

Jim raised a questioning eyebrow when Harry looked over at him.

"He died. Our baby died."

He took a swig from the beer bottle.

"It was Libby who found him. In his cot."

"How old was he?"

"Four months and six days."

Harry paused again.

"I was at work. Libby phoned me in hysterics. By the time I got home, the ambulance was there. They took him away. There was a funeral. That was that."

Harry glanced at Jim.

"Didn't Libby tell you all this?"

Jim shook his head.

"So what did she tell you?"

"Not much, really. It's how she's behaved that's told us anything, while we've been travelling."

"Tell me how you met Libby."

"We were all meeting up in a car park, across in Canterbury. We usually meet there because it's easy to get onto the motorway and on to Dover for the ferry. Anyway, I got there early, before anyone else, and I just sat in the van and had a smoke while I waited for the others. When I first got there I noticed a woman sitting on the wall at the edge of the car park. She was on her own, just sitting there, looking about, like she was waiting for someone. I remember thinking that she seemed a little agitated, like something was urgent. Well, after about twenty minutes, my mates arrived, and as we chatted I noticed that she was still there. She wasn't really doing anything, just waiting.

"We all got ready to go and set off out of the car park. I was the last one to leave, and just as I started the engine and began to move, she suddenly got up and ran across to the van. I braked hard because I thought she might run in front of me, but she didn't."

"What did she do?"

"She banged and banged hard on my window and shouted for me to take her with me."

"What - she just wanted to get in the van and go, with a total stranger?"

"Yes. I wound the window down, and asked her what was wrong, and if I could help. She just kept asking me if she could come along. She said she wouldn't be any trouble, she just had to get away."

Harry looked confused.

"I wasn't sure what to do, but it all seemed so urgent that I relented and she jumped into the passenger seat."

"You shouldn't have done that," was all Harry said.

"I know, but looking back, I'm glad I did. Anyway, as we drove the first few miles she just sat in silence, staring ahead. I wondered what was wrong, of course. I thought that maybe she was running away from something sinister - you know, like a prostitution ring.........................."

Harry snorted sarcastically but Jim chose to ignore him.

".....................or a dodgy husband. In the end she was right, she wasn't being any trouble, and we just drove on. When we stopped at the services, she got on OK with the others I was travelling with. It all seemed easy after that. She had a passport with her and a bit of money. She bought a ticket for the ferry when we got to Dover, and then we were all off to France."

"I've got lots of postcards at home," Harry said simply.

"I know. She didn't say anything about you, but she always wanted to send you a postcard whenever we stopped."

"What have you been doing, out in Europe?"

"Oh, this and that. Some of us do a bit of street entertaining - you know, acrobatics, juggling, stuff like that. We find jobs in bars, or fruit picking, if we need extra money. We do this every summer. It's great."

"Really?"

Jim knew Harry was being sarcastic again. He leaned forward.

"Look - Libby obviously had to get away from something, and all I did was give her that chance."

Jim looked across the field.

"Here she comes. I'll get out of the way. And careful - she's fragile."

Jim disappeared round the other side of the van, leaving Harry alone to watch Libby as she approached. Harry suddenly felt sick, but he knew he had to face her. Libby stopped in her tracks when she noticed Harry. She stared at him, frozen, as if she'd seen a ghost, and Harry was ashamed that she looked so frightened of him. He'd expected her to either run away again, attack him out of anger, or start an argument. She did none of these things. Instead, she just stared at him. Eventually, Harry stepped forward and reached a hand out to her.

"Libby........................."

Libby shrank back from him, so Harry stepped backwards again.

"It's OK, it's OK. Don't worry. I'll stay right over here."

Harry indicated to an imaginary line in front of him, a boundary between them, that he wouldn't cross. He smiled. Still Libby said nothing.

"I got your postcards. I've got them all on the wall in the study. You've been to lots of places, haven't you? You and your friends?"

"Stop treating me like a child. I didn't expect to see you here," Libby finally spoke, matter-of-factly.

"Yes, well. I've missed you, and............when I saw a chance to come and find you, I took it."

Harry was finding the conversation difficult, and Libby wasn't helping.

"So, they let you have time off work, to come down here?"

"Yes," Harry laughed a small uncomfortable laugh. "Well, I would have come anyway."

"Would you? Why?"

"Libby - to see you, of course."

Libby paused. Harry groaned inside when he realized that he knew what she was going to say before she said it.

"Really?" Libby's voice was raised. "There was a time, fifteen months ago, when I called you and asked you to come home. From the office."

Harry looked around uncomfortably.

"Yes, Libby. I know. I've never forgotten that."

"That was the day I left."

Harry looked away. Quietly he said, "I'd like the chance to put that right."

When Harry looked back at Libby, she was crying quietly. He reached out to her.

"Libby, please.................."

But in an instant Libby was gone. She turned and ran round the corner of the van, and away across the field.

"Damn!" Harry snapped to himself.

Just then, Jim appeared again.

"How'd it go?" he asked.

"She's different. She's changed."

"Things that happen to us make us change," was Jim's reply.

"I don't know what to do."

Jim felt a little sorry for Harry. He guessed that people didn't usually challenge his routine or his view of the world like this.

"Don't do anything. Leave it alone and see what happens."

"That makes me feel helpless," Harry replied.

Jim shrugged.

"Maybe you are."

"Thanks."

"Look - why don't you go back to where you're staying. Give me the address, and I'll call round in a bit. How does that sound?"

"Do I have a choice?"

Harry found an old receipt in his pocket and scribbled down his mobile number, and Mrs Matthews' address and phone number. He handed it to Jim.

"Thanks," Jim said as he stuffed it in his pocket.

"I'll be off, then."

Harry turned to set off back to his car.

"Oh, and Harry........."

Harry turned back.

"Yes?"

Jim swung hard and knocked Harry to the ground, where he lay, dazed and confused, staring at Jim.

"Don't ever hit me again," said Jim, and he walked away.

That evening, Harry sat in the corner of a bar, staring into his pint and speaking to no-one. He allowed himself to get used to his new situation. At least he'd found Libby. That was a start, after the long silence of the last fifteen months. But how to persuade her to come home? He was on new ground there. When he lived with Libby before she ran off, she was very compliant, easy to get round, did what he asked. A nasty feeling came over him as he realized for the first time that he may not have been the good husband he thought he was, that he may not have looked after Libby, may have been unfeeling as she needed to grieve for their baby. Just as he considered sinking another pint - his way of dealing with all of this - his mobile phone rang. He answered it quickly.

"Hello, yes?"

"Harry? It's Jim."

"Hang on. I'll go outside. Signal's bad."

Harry sat on a bench in the beer garden and listened patiently to Jim.

"I've had a chat with Libby. She says it gave her quite a fright to see you there. She wasn't expecting it."

"OK. What else?"

"Well, I've persuaded her to let you come over and stay on the campsite. I've got a small tent we can put up next to the van. Then I think it's between you two, to sort things out."

Harry was quiet.

"Harry? Are you there?"

"Yes. I just thought she.........oh, never mind."

"So, you want to come over? Now? Or some time tomorrow?"

"I'll come over tomorrow."

"Right. Well, we've got our street show in the high street at twelve. You could come and watch it and then follow us back."

"What street show?"

"Me and Libby, doing stuff. Acrobatics, comedy, juggling. You know. I told you, that's what we've been doing in Europe."

"OK, OK. I'll come and find you then."

"Right - and make sure you put some money in the hat!"

Jim laughed. Harry didn't.

"See you tomorrow, Harry. Oh, and Harry - say 'thanks, Jim.'"

"Thanks, Jim."

Jim laughed again.

"See you tomorrow."

Harry walked back to the B'n'B and slept peacefully, better than he had for a long time, probably for about fifteen months.

*   *   *

Next morning, it was bright and sunny. Harry woke and had breakfast early, then packed his things and said goodbye to Mrs Matthews. She seemed cross he was leaving, but Harry didn't care. He put his suitcase in the boot of his car, parked up in the public car park in the town centre, and then set off to find Jim's street show. Harry remembered that there was some sort of festival going on. As he walked along the high street, he passed wooden stalls selling a variety of goods. There was a small music stage in one of the side streets, and a larger stage in the town centre. The sun was getting hotter and hotter as he walked, and the crowds were already making it difficult to get by. Eventually Harry noticed a crowd collecting round something on the street corner. When he investigated closer, he saw Jim and Libby warming up, jumping and stretching, getting ready to perform. He decided to stay anonymous for the moment, and he mingled with the crowd. Finally the show started. Jim walked around the edge of the performance area that had been created naturally as the crowd gathered, and he smiled at everyone.

"Ladies and gentlemen, boys and girls, you are going to watch the best street show you'll see anywhere in the world at this point in time. Are you ready for acrobatics?"

Jim paused in his delivery and held his hand to his ear, waiting for a response. He waved his hand in a beckoning fashion and everyone clapped and cheered. Behind him, Libby smiled to herself.

"That's better," he continued. "Now, are you ready for a bit of dancing, some daring acrobatics, and the finale, our daring, dangerous fire juggling!"

This time the crowd clapped and cheered without any prompt from Jim.

"Right then, off we go!"

Jim bounced across to a huge CD player and set the music away.

A loud regular drumbeat, with a rap across the top, boomed across the town centre. People immediately started to clap in time to it. Jim and Libby got together in the middle, counted themselves in, and then began a hip-hop type of dance routine. After a while they became more adventurous, and Libby started to run and jump across their performance space. People applauded loudly. Harry was surprised to find that he was impressed.

Finally, Jim produced four fire clubs. He gave Libby two and kept the other two. Libby lit each club and they held them up high for the audience to see. Jim looked round the excited crowd.

"Ladies and gentlemen, boys and girls, are you enjoying the show?" A loud response from the crowd said 'yes'.

"And now for our grand finale - our fire juggling act. Watch out at the front. We don't want to singe your hair!"

Everyone laughed. Jim changed the music on the tape to a loud, ethnic track reminiscent of Moroccan street markets or Egyptian dancing. He looked at Libby, who was concentrating hard. He counted in, and together they juggled their fire clubs. The flames moved in symmetry, leaving hypnotic traces of light in the air. Everyone gasped.

"Are you watching carefully?" Jim shouted as he watched his

clubs. "Ready?"

Suddenly, Libby and Jim combined juggling their clubs with passing them to each other. Again, the well-rehearsed symmetry of the movement impressed the crowd. Jim and Libby carried on like this for a minute or so, and then stopped together, blew out the clubs and bowed to the audience. Everyone cheered.

"Thank you, thank you. And now my beautiful assistant Libby will pass among you with my lucky hat, which has the special gift of being able to fill with money when it knows it is close to the best and most generous of folks."

Again everyone laughed, and people put change and notes in the hat as Libby held it out around the crowd. People waved goodbye as they set off in search of further entertainment, and left Harry standing alone, watching Libby and Jim.

Jim looked up at Harry as he packed his things away in a rucksack.

"Hey, Harry."

Libby also looked at Harry, but she didn't speak to him.

"We put the tent up for you," Jim continued. "Where's your car?"

"Over there, in that car park."

"We'll wait here for you in the van, then you can follow us."

"OK." Harry paused, then remembered to say "Thanks."

*   *   *

Next morning, Harry was reminded about why he'd never really gone in for camping, when he woke with a stiff back from lying uncomfortably on the stony ground. This made him grumpy as he considered his situation. He'd hoped to spend some time with Libby alone, to talk, but she had done a good job of avoiding him during the previous evening.

As the sun gradually began to warm up the inside of the tent while he lay there, he heard Jim's van door open and then close again. He continued to lie there, expecting Jim or Libby to call him or tap on the tent door. Nothing happened, so he unzipped the top of the door and looked out. To his surprise and irritation, he just caught sight of Jim and Libby as they climbed over a stile in the hedge and walked into the woods. It was only six-thirty. What were they doing going anywhere so early? He dressed quickly and set off after them, keeping back so they wouldn't know he was there.

Harry followed Jim and Libby to a clearing a little way in, with a pond in the middle. They were sitting down together on an overturned tree trunk and talking quietly. Harry was too far away to catch what they were talking about. To his surprise, Libby got up and walked off into the trees, while Jim watched her. What was Libby doing? She seemed to be examining different trees, studying and feeling each trunk, and looking up at how far each one disappeared into the sky overhead. Meanwhile, Jim just sat still and smoked his roll-up. Eventually Libby turned and came back to join Jim, so Harry turned and headed back to the campsite. He felt confused by what he'd just seen. He realized he also felt a little disappointed; he thought he was about to see some evidence that Jim and Libby were more than friends after all. Then he felt relieved that they weren't. So many feelings, so many confusions. He climbed back into his tent and tried to go back to sleep.

Later that morning Harry emerged from the tent. He discovered Jim sitting in the back of his van. He was boiling a kettle.

"Hey. Sleep alright?" he grinned.

"So so," Harry replied.

"Come in and have a cuppa."

"Thanks."

Harry climbed in and sat on the bed opposite Jim - Libby's bed. He felt strange, as if he was being invasive.

"Where's Libby?"

Jim indicated across the field with his spoon.

"Having breakfast with Jill, over there."

"Has she said anything?"

"About what?"

Harry grew impatient.

"About me, of course. Me and her. What's happening."

"No."

Harry watched Jim pour hot water into two mugs.

"Sugar?"

"No, thank you. Just milk."

Harry eyed Jim suspiciously as he passed his mug across to him. They sat in silence.

"I don't know what to do next, Jim."

"Nor me. Best to just be around. Let Libby trust you. Then you can talk."

"Are you saying my wife doesn't trust me?"

"Well, frankly, yes. Otherwise she wouldn't be avoiding you."

Harry was becoming angry again. He couldn't help pulling out his trump card.

"I saw you this morning."

"Who - me?"

"No - you and Libby. I followed you into the trees."

"Bit naughty, that was, Harry."

"Why?"

"Because that's Libby private space, the early mornings."

Harry sat in silence, confused by Jim's response. Jim leaned forward a little, indicating that he wanted to speak a bit quieter.

"Listen. Remember when I said that Libby never told us about the baby, and that it was her behaviour that explained what was going on?"

Harry nodded.

"Well, every time we've stopped, all over Europe, Libby wanted to find a tree."

"What are you talking about? You don't have to look hard to find a tree! They're all over the place."

Jim paused as he was reminded that Harry saw the world very differently to himself. Very black and white, straight down the line. Poor Harry couldn't think in a broader way, Jim decided.

"Yes, but not just any tree. Libby likes to get up early, when no-one's about, and look for the right tree."

"You're not making sense, Jim. Explain, please."

Jim paused before he continued and drank some of his tea.

"Don't you see, Harry? Libby looks for the right tree, and only she understands what that means. No-one else. And then she carves a name in the tree."

Harry stared at Jim. "He doesn't get it," Jim thought to himself.

"Libby carves the name 'Luke' on the tree. That's how we knew she was probably dealing with a grief. There are trees all over Europe with the name Luke on them. They're helping Libby to keep Luke's memory alive. Don't ask me why. It's just her way...........her way of doing things."

Harry stared past Jim and out into the sunshine. He said nothing.

"That's why I told you to be careful. She's still fragile, because she still wants to find another tree, for Luke."

There was an awkward silence now.

"You might have come along at just the right time, Harry, or you might not. Only time will tell, but Libby has to run the show."

Harry suddenly put his mug down, climbed out of the van without looking at Jim, and walked away to a corner of the field, where he stood alone. Jim guessed he was probably having some private tears, and he knew this was what Harry needed.

*   *   *

At lunchtime, everyone sat together in the middle of the field, while Libby and a couple of other girls cooked a barbecue. To Harry's surprise, Libby put two burgers in buns and brought them across to him. As Harry watched Libby approach he told himself to get it right.

"Here you are," Libby said.

"Thank you."

Libby turned to go.

"Libby - wait. Please."

Libby hesitated, but did turn back. She looked expectantly at Harry.

"Er..........I wondered if we could spend some time on our own."

Harry paused. Libby did not respond.

"I'd really like to talk to you, about everything."

Don't mention trees, Harry was telling himself. You're stupid and you always open your big mouth.

"Maybe later," was all Libby said. She seemed to manage a smile at the corner of her mouth, and then she walked away. Harry felt frustrated, but he tried to remember what Jim had said; let Libby run the show.

"Hey, Harry!"

Jim called across to Harry, pulling him out of his daydream. Harry got up and went over to Jim.

"Libby and I are collecting today. It's Jill's turn to do her act in town, with Steve and Pete. They do this comedy thing. Wanna come?"

"OK."

"Come with us in the van."

An hour later, the traveller friends were back in the street in Coleford, getting ready for Jill's show. Harry watched from a distance as Jim hooked up a microphone to a small amp and tested it with the usual 'one, two'. Pete, Steve and Jill were off in the corner tuning up instruments - a fiddle and two guitars. Harry had to admit that he was looking forward to seeing this act and how they would make it funny. Finally the show began. Jill stepped up to the microphone, which Jim had placed on a stand on the pavement, and started to sing a song about a farmer and his wife. Her thin wispy voice suited the ballad she sent out across the street, and people soon stopped to crowd around and listen. However, the words of the song began to deviate into a funnier plot about what the farmer's wife was going to do when she caught up with him, and soon everyone was roaring with laughter. This first song was a prelude to a comedy musical show, which had the audience in stitches for the next twenty minutes. Harry knew the end was coming when he saw Jim and Libby start to move around the audience with upturned hats, gently haggling people for a bigger and bigger donation.

Suddenly, everything changed. One moment Libby was mingling with the crowd, the next moment Harry saw her drop the hat, coins flying everywhere, and she swayed a little on her feet as if in shock. She stared through the crowd, watching something, and then she darted away down the street. Jim was quicker than Harry. He'd also seen Libby leave, and ran straight after her. In the chaos that followed, Jill, Pete and Steve tried to retrieve their takings before the local kids got them, and Harry was off down the street after his wife.

He found Libby and Jim in the car park by the library. She was sobbing and shaking, while Jim held her tight.

"What happened? What's wrong?" Harry shouted as he ran up to them. Jim waved him away and held onto Libby. This rejection made

Harry angry, but before he could speak, Libby burst into hysterics.

"It was the same little boy, Jim. The one I saw in the woods. He was watching me through the crowd."

"Ssssh," Jim said soothingly. "I told you, he must live here or be on holiday with his family."

Harry listened as Libby continued.

"But Jim, this time he caught my eye and when he knew I was looking, he beckoned to me. Did you hear me? He waved at me that I was to follow him. And now I can't see him anywhere. Where's he gone?"

Jim finally turned to Harry. His face was full of grim concern. Something gradually dawned on Harry; the words the spiritualist had told him. 'Tell Harry that he will find everything he needs, here in the forest.' Harry looked at Libby, his own head starting to spin, and he turned and walked away.

* * *

Harry sat on a bench in the park. He sat there for two hours, deep in thought. He didn't know anything about Libby seeing a little boy in the woods until today, and then she'd seen him again in the crowd. He had gone over and over Libby's words and he knew what her distress was about. There was a magic in the air, something he couldn't explain. There was a question driving his thoughts. The spiritualist's words went round and round in his head. Libby's words mingled with them and, combined, they gave him his answer; Libby believed that she was seeing their son. Harry looked at his watch. Quarter to seven. He stood up, stretched the stiffness in his legs away and set off into town.

Mrs Matthews opened the door before he knocked.

"Harry! How nice to see you. You've come for our Thursday evening meeting, I hope?"

"If that's alright."

"Of course it is. Come on in."

Harry followed Mrs Matthews into the lounge. He saw the same group of people, sitting together around the coffee table. Harry saw Jack, who had given him his message two days earlier. Jack stood up and extended his hand.

"Hello, Harry. Nice to see you again."

Jack shook Harry's hand firmly.

"Here. Have a seat."

Harry sat down next to Jack and then wondered what to do next. He was feeling so apprehensive that he felt like running out again, but he breathed deeply and tried to stay calm.

The meeting began formally with a meditation and a couple of prayers, during which Harry felt bored and sleepy. Next, Mrs Matthews announced the 'open circle', in which anyone could share their messages. Various members of the group spoke, bringing information from their 'spiritual' sources. Some of it was vague and general, while some bits were more specific. Harry found that his attention started to wander and he began to daydream - about Libby, trees, small boys, work and postcards. In his mind's eye, he had a sudden image of his mother, and what she would say when he told her he was chasing around the country after his errant wife instead of working hard. This thought brought him back to the meeting with a jolt, because he remembered that his mother had been dead for three years. Someone was nudging his elbow. It was Jack. Harry turned and looked at him.

"Sylvia has something for you," Jack said solemnly, and nodded across the coffee table at an elderly lady. Sylvia smiled.

"On Tuesday, Jack told you that everything you needed was here. You knew this even before you set off from home."

"My wife," Harry said quietly.

"Yes," Sylvia continued. "And also some knowledge that has been given to you. This can happen in a spiritual place like our forest, where the trees and the water and the huge expanse of nature makes us feel small and insignificant next to that greater power."

Harry wasn't sure what Sylvia meant. He only realized that he hadn't really taken any notice of the 'trees and the water and the huge expanse of nature'. He had focused on speaking to Libby.

"Now listen carefully, because you may find this hard."

Harry felt himself stiffen, ready for bad news. Sylvia looked at him directly and seriously.

"We all have a certain amount of time here, and we all have a purpose. You've probably heard the phrase 'everything happens for a reason'."

Harry nodded.

"When someone dies, we cannot always see the reason or the purpose, but both things are still there. If we allow ourselves the space and time to consider these greater questions, we become stronger, calmer and more tolerant."

Harry was hoping for a message, not a lot of flannel and philosophy.

"Your baby, Luke, had only a short time here."

Tears sprang up in Harry's eyes and he wiped them away.

"Even so, he had his own reason and purpose for the time he spent with you."

"What does that mean?" Harry spoke out.

"Only you know that answer. He was part of your life, not mine. But you could ask yourself, Harry, what would things have been like if Luke had stayed here?"

Harry realized that he'd never given this idea much thought.

"Libby would still be at home with me," he said. "She wouldn't have run off like she did."

Sylvia leaned forward. She smiled.

"Luke is with us now, standing over by the armchair."

Harry looked but couldn't see anything.

"Such a beautiful child. He says to tell you: are you quite sure that what you just said is true?"

Harry stared at Sylvia. What was she talking about?

He felt himself withdraw, become small inside the sofa he was sitting on, and confused thoughts stayed with him as he sat through the rest of the meeting without speaking. When the meeting ended with more prayers and a moment of silence, Harry declined to stay for the tea and biscuits and quickly left. He found a taxi and went back to the campsite.

*   *   *

The taxi dropped Harry off at the entrance to the campsite, and when he walked into the field, Harry found it deserted. The various vans and tents were closed up. No fires or barbecues were burning brightly in the middle. Bemused, Harry walked over to his tent and found a note pinned to the door. The note was from Jim, letting Harry know that they'd all gone to the pub up the road, where there was an open mike session that evening. Harry didn't know what an 'open mike' session was, but it sounded better than sitting around on his own waiting for them to come back. He changed into some jeans and a T-shirt, which seemed more 'pub like', and set off down the road. After a couple of bends in the winding road, the pub loomed up in front of him. It was a typical country pub, painted white with ivy growing everywhere. As Harry got closer he could hear the live music from somewhere round the back. Harry walked in through the front door and found himself in a long bar. The place was packed, and at one end there was a raised wooden platform, which served as a stage. A man with a guitar had just finished his song and the crowd clapped enthusiastically. Harry bought a pint of local beer and then looked around for Jim, Libby and the others. He found them outside.

The group of friends were sitting on the grass, playing a variety of instruments, tuning up and trying out ideas. Harry felt awkward as he approached them, but Jim waved. Libby watched Harry as well, but still said nothing.

"Where did you get to?" Jim called.

"Oh, just off on my own for a bit. Thinking time," Harry replied, and he glanced at Libby. She caught his eye and looked away.

"Wanna game of pool?" Jim continued. "No-one else will play me. I'm too good."

"I've never played pool," Harry admitted.

"Even better, then," laughed Jim. "We'll play winner stays on."

Harry knocked back his pint and quickly bought another. He was rubbish at pool, and Jim patiently tried to help him improve. Harry didn't care about the pool. He was suddenly in a mood for throwing caution to the winds and getting drunk; something he couldn't remember ever doing. Jim, drinking at half Harry's speed, raised an eyebrow.

"You sure you're alright?"

"Fine. Just fine. Your break."

Harry's game gradually got worse, if it possibly could, and he started to wobble about as he moved around the pool table. Jim wasn't sure where this might be heading, when suddenly Libby appeared with a guitar.

"Jim - will you tune my guitar for me, please? I can go up next and do a song."

"Cool," said Jim, and tuned the guitar. Libby looked across at Harry, buying another drink at the bar.

"He's having a few," Jim commented.

"Do him good," Libby replied, and disappeared into the crowd.

"Was that Libby?" Harry slurred when he came back.

"Certainly was. She's going to sing next. Let's stop playing and listen, eh?"

Jim and Harry sat by the pool table and watched as Libby climbed up onto the stage and sat on the stool by the microphone.

"I didn't know Libby could play the guitar," Harry shouted above the noise.

"Well, she can't, really. I tune it differently for her so she doesn't have to play real chords. She just moves her hand up and down the neck in one position. She's written a few nice songs, though, while we've been travelling."

Harry wasn't sure how to react to Jim's information, so he sat quiet. Gradually the crowd settled down to listen, and Libby began to strum the guitar. Harry realized that he'd never heard Libby sing, and when her gentle, folky voice began to spread across the bar, he was touched. He listened, gazing into his pint, as Libby sang about pain and loss and hope and lots of other emotions in between. Harry suddenly took the song as a sign from her to him. He thought back to Sylvia's words, and they made sense. He had chased Libby away. He hadn't helped her when she needed him. She'd found more support from a bunch of travelling entertainers, when it should have come from him. He realized that there was a side to Libby that he didn't know at all, and that was what Luke's message meant. If Luke hadn't died, what would their life have been like? Him at the office, winning all the sales awards, with a stereotype wife and son on display. Harry thought about all these things and he felt ashamed. He burst into tears and fell weeping onto Jim's shoulder. Jim jumped when Harry fell onto him, because he was looking the other way and watching Libby, but he saw the pain in Harry's face and he did the only thing he could - he hugged him in a 'manly' hug and let him cry. No-one around them laughed. People seemed to understand that Harry needed to do this, because this was the forest and it was full of magic. At the end of the evening, Jim, Pete and Steve helped Harry back to his tent and put him to bed. In the morning, when Jim called through the tent door and woke him at six o'clock, Harry couldn't remember how he got there.

*   *   *

When Harry climbed out of the tent, Libby was waiting with Jim.

"Hello," Harry laughed nervously. "It's early."

To his complete surprise, Libby answered him.

"Come for a walk with me, Harry."

"Alright. Where to?"

Libby pointed over the stile, while Harry struggled to clear his head. Jim produced a cup of black coffee and passed it to Harry.

"Thanks. Sorry about last night."

"No problem. Think you needed to let us look after you."

Harry knocked back the coffee quickly, since Libby seemed anxious to get on, and they set off across the field. He turned back to Jim.

"Aren't you coming?"

"No. Not today."

Jim winked at Harry and then climbed back into his van. Libby had already reached the stile and Harry hurried after her.

One at a time they climbed over the stile and then set off together into the trees. They walked in silence, Libby leading the way, Harry following behind. As they walked, Harry felt that he was looking at everything in a new light. He saw the mist hanging amongst the branches, heard birds as they called to each other. They arrived at the pond and Harry noticed the stillness, the calmness of the clearing and the atmospheric effect of the dark, deep water. Once in the clearing, Libby stopped. Harry watched as she stared across the clearing into the trees ahead. He looked at her dyed red hair, the shape of her shoulders under her T-shirt, remembered the colour of her eyes, and he realized that it was a long, long time since he had told Libby that he loved her.

"Libby, I.................." he began.

"Sssh," Libby whispered, holding up her hand to silence Harry in mid-sentence.

There was an awkward pause, then Libby spoke without looking at Harry.

"I've been very angry with you," she said.

"I know. And I know why. I'm sorry."

"You remember, we met at college and then we got married, and I didn't do anything."

Harry spoke cautiously.

"I thought you were happy with that, being at home, being with me."

"Then Luke came along and filled my days," Libby continued, "and it was only after he left again, that I realized what my life was about. I had

55

nothing."

Tears filled Harry's eyes.

"Oh, Libby. Don't say you had nothing. We can have another....."

Libby turned to Harry and shot a glance that told him not to finish what he was about to say. He paused before he spoke again.

"Libby - please come home with me. I'm lost without you."

Libby waited, considering what Harry had just said.

"We went over the top of the Pyrenees, in the van. Right over the peak. It was so high we were in the clouds, and we stopped to have a look across the view."

"It must have been beautiful," Harry whispered.

"More than that, Harry," Libby became more animated now. "Much more than that. It was spiritual, full of meaning, full of the space that surrounds us, space that isn't full of clutter and bills and jobs and cooking and housework. I'd never been to anywhere that made me feel like that."

"No," Harry replied, almost mournfully.

"And I found other places along the way that made me feel the same. High mountains, rushing rivers, huge churches, deep caves, and I realized that I wanted more. I wanted to see more places that made me feel so at peace. And I knew that losing Luke had got me there, so I promised I wouldn't forget that. I have carved his name on so many trees around Europe, so people might walk past and see his name, and wonder who he is and what he did to have his name on that tree. Luke saved me, Harry, he gave me a chance to be me. Can't you see that?"

Harry nodded, and looked very sad.

"Please come home," he said again.

"Are you missing the point deliberately, or can you just not see what I'm saying?"

Harry looked Libby straight in the eye.

"Do you love me?" he asked quietly.

"Of course I love you! Why do you think I sent you all those postcards? I wanted to see you again, Harry, but I don't want our old life."

Harry began to cry, and Libby looked back towards the trees. She ignored Harry as he wept next to her, and walked towards a particular tree, a tall slim larch that spread its fingers up to the sky. She looked up the tree into the highest branches, then turned to Harry.

"This one," she said, as she took a penknife out of her pocket and held it towards him. Harry walked over to join Libby, took the knife from her, paused while he examined the tree bark, and then began to hack away at it. Libby watched while Harry became more determined in his task, and he soon carved the letters L U K E into the wood. He turned to look at Libby. She looked very serious.

"Come with me, Harry."

"Where to?"

"Don't know yet. I just want to keep going."

Harry thought about what he would leave behind - the house, the office, the boys at work - and he thought about Jack's message one more time. 'Tell Harry that he will find everything he needs, here in the forest.'

"OK," he said quietly.

Libby sighed and turned back towards the path. Harry followed her, hoping he'd said the right thing, and they walked in silence back to the stile. Harry saw Jim waiting by the van as they headed back across the field. He knew Jim wanted to know what had happened. Harry thought he would reach out and take Libby's hand; a sign for everyone watching.

Before he had time to do this, Libby suddenly reached out herself and took Harry's hand. He held on tight, never letting go again, and allowed himself to look forward to a future without plans, without targets, without meetings, without expectations, just him and his wife, somewhere, and together.

The Hill

The right people and the wrong people lived on either side of a high hill. The hill was so steep, there were no obvious paths to allow anyone to traverse its peak and reach the other side. The sides of the hill were loose and slippery, and covered in shale, mud and rotting leaves, so over the years everyone from both villages had gradually avoided any attempts to use the hill as part of their daily route.

At some time in the past, in spite of this geographical difficulty, the right people and the wrong people had somehow managed to have a falling out. No-one alive knew what this disagreement had been about, since it had been so long ago, but everyone knew that it was forbidden to contact the people in the other village, whether you fancied you could climb the hill to get there, or spend the considerable time it would take to walk the long way round.

*   *   *

Matty was three years old. Her happy and contented daily life involved playing all day. She could spend hours making small cities for her wooden dolls in the mud, chasing butterflies, or wrestling with the huge family dog. The only thing she had to remember was her mother's one strict rule; Matty could never, ever leave the garden. Because this didn't seem unreasonable, it was a simple rule to adhere to. Her mother, Thea, would spend her day busy with chores, as the cooking, cleaning and washing was never-ending. Thea's husband Jacob would be out all day, hunting or working in their family plot in the fields around the village. Animals had to be taken to market, tools had to be fixed. The work never ended, and all the while they worked, they knew that Matty was safe within her domestic boundary. They seemed happy and content, and no-one moaned about their lot.

However, if Matty had the awareness that was surely to come as she grew older, she would have realised that all was not right with the world, that there was something wrong with the seeming domestic bliss, and that she - Matty - was the cause. Jacob and Thea had been married for some years now, and had never been blessed with a child. Now in middle age, Thea was never expected to conceive. She knew that the popular view in the village was that it was Thea's lot in life to remain one of the childless. So when Thea discovered that she was pregnant, a dark cloud entered the family home.

A child born in this stage of her life, when such possibilities should have passed, must surely be a sign of bad luck. Thea and Jacob knew that this was the belief that was generally held in the village, and gradually they came to believe it themselves. By the time the child arrived, and should have been a much wanted and cherished only daughter, Thea felt no bonding with her baby, and Jacob felt helpless and confused. Try as he might, he found his own feelings following fast behind those of Thea's, and the best he could offer Matty was a kind of affectionate security; don't leave the garden, where you're safe.

If Matty was happily unaware of this shadow in her daily life, then she must have known something was wrong deep in her subconscious, because on the day she cut her finger on a sharp twig at the bottom of the garden, she didn't tell anyone. Matty had lost interest in playing with her toys, and the dog had run off somewhere, so she had begun exploring at the very end of the garden. She saw something bright in the hedge, and discovered some pretty wild flowers growing there. Thinking that she could pick them and give them to her mother, she reached in and snagged her tiny forefinger on the sharp thorns. Matty pulled her hand back quickly and watched curiously as deep red blood seeped from the cut. It wasn't really painful, and Matty was more interested in what happened if she squeezed her finger, which made the blood come out quicker, or if she sucked on it, which seemed to make it stop. The thing she didn't expect was that as she watched, the cut slowly began to disappear. The skin seemed to move across the cut, knit together and leave a tiny scar. Matty was intrigued. Something deep inside her told her that her finger shouldn't have healed so quickly, and something deeper again told her not to mention any of this to her mother.

The next few days passed in harmful play, and Matty might have forgotten about the whole business, except that her natural childish curiosity made her decide that she wanted to see if the same thing would happen again. She crept into the kitchen, where Thea was baking bread, and she watched Thea kneading the dough hard on the large wooden table, watched her stop now and then to wipe her brow. Matty knew there was always a fire lit in the hearth, even if it was just a small one, to use for heating water at least, and this is what she was interested in. While her mother's back was turned, Matty crept up to the fire and slowly reached into it. She knew it would be hot - she knew that much already - and she placed the palm of her hand just close enough to feel it burn, then she quickly pulled it away again. She looked at her hand. Her palm was red and swollen; a large blister was beginning to blossom outwards. She was just about to put her hand in the pocket of her apron, when Thea appeared behind her, grabbed her arm roughly and pulled her up onto her feet.

"What are you doing?" Thea cried, shaking Matty by her arm. "You know you shouldn't go near the fire."

Thea instantly felt guilty. She stopped shaking Matty, picked her up and sat her on the edge of the table.

"What were you doing?"

Matty stared at her mother in silence.

"What were you doing near the fire? Answer me."

Matty opened her hand flat, palm up, so that her mother could see the burn.

"Foolish child. Now look at your hand."

Thea stopped herself, realising that she probably sounded too unsympathetic.

"Let's put some cold water on it, at least."

Thea left her daughter sitting on the table while she fetched a cloth and a jug of water.

"Here," she began, "Hold out your hand again and I'll................"

Thea stared at her daughter's hand. She checked it, turning it over and over.

"But Matty, where's the burn? It was here. I saw it."

"It got better," Matty whispered. "By itself."

When Thea examined Matty's hand more closely she saw that the burn had indeed healed completely, leaving only a lighter patch of new skin which would probably become a scar. Thea stared at her daughter.

"My finger got better as well. By itself."

"When?"

"When I was playing."

Matty showed Thea her finger. Suddenly, Thea burst into an anguished tirade.

"Oh, no. Oh, Matty. What will your father say? This is not a good sign."

She looked at Matty, who was swinging her legs in the air, and pointed at Matty's tiny hand.

"What does that mean? Why did your hand get better by itself?"

Thea suddenly checked herself, remembering that she was talking to a child, three years old, who wouldn't know the answer to this question. One thing Matty gleaned from her mother's reaction, though, was a new feeling; a feeling that there was definitely something wrong about all this, and that this made her mother afraid.

"Matty. You must promise me something, alright?"

Matty nodded. Thea bent down to Matty's eye level and gently took her hands in hers.

"Let's keep this a secret, just between you and me. Something for just us two girls to know about, and we'll not tell your father."

"Why?" Matty asked.

"Because," her mother paused before continuing, choosing her words carefully, "I don't think he's ever heard of a thing like this happening to anyone before, and he may think well, why does Matty have some sort of special thing happening to her, and I don't!"

Thea smiled, to lighten the moment. She hoped that she was catching her daughter's interest, drawing her into her devious plan by making it seem like a game. The truth was, she was frightened of what she had just witnessed, and Matty's place in the family home and in the village, as a 'weird child', would only be confirmed if this got out.

"Can you keep this a secret?" Thea whispered.

Matty nodded solemnly.

"Good. And I will too. Now, do you want to help me finish the bread?"

*　　　　*　　　　*

Over the next few weeks, Thea made efforts to watch her daughter more carefully. This was solely because she didn't want to give Matty the opportunity to share her secret with anyone, more than out of any changes in her motherly instincts towards her. For her part, Matty noticed the change in Thea's vigilance, and she felt stifled by it. She began to make a game of disappearing from view at intervals. She would lie down behind the dog, or hide under her bed, or climb up into a tree, and then enjoy the stress it caused Thea when she had to put down whatever she was doing and look for Matty. Then one day, Matty decided to go one step further.

That morning, she watched while her mother struggled to hang out the washing in a particularly strong breeze. When the wind suddenly whipped up the dress Thea was trying to hang out, and wrapped it in a knot around her, Matty saw her chance. In an instant she was at the bottom of the garden, through the hole in the hedge, and then off across the fields. She looked back once and saw her mother still struggling with the dress, which looked like it had taken on a life of its own, not allowing itself to simply hang on the line, when it could be having fun billowing about in the open air around Thea's head. Matty laughed and ran on.

Up ahead, Matty could see the huge hill stretching away in front of her. She had looked at this hill on most days during her short life, and wondered who or what lived in the thick forest which covered the hill as far as she could see. Now she wanted to explore it. Matty walked on, determined by nature and too young to be afraid, and soon she came to the end of the fields, where the occasional tree marked the start of the dark, uninviting wood. Once in the thick of the trees, Matty found the going much harder. The ground quickly grew too steep for her to walk up, and she found herself slipping and sliding in the undergrowth, grabbing at ferns and tree roots to pull herself up, and then frequently missing them and sliding down the way she'd just climbed. However, Matty wasn't worried. She just concentrated on going upwards. The feeling she was experiencing, although too young to put a name to it, was freedom; being out in the open space.

Matty stopped now and then to look around. She was surrounded on all sides by tall trees. Their thin, silvery trunks reached up into the sky as far as Matty could see, their branches rustled and swayed in the wind above her head and their dead leaves, cast down in seasons long past, made a thick brown carpet on the ground. Matty became dizzy from the looking up, and sat down for a moment. That was when she noticed the shelter.

Matty stared at the shelter, which lay ahead of her on her upward route. At first she was unsure whether or not to investigate, but then she set off towards it. When she got close, she found that the shelter was round in shape, and someone had made it by bending a series of long thin branches, then pushing the ends into the ground to hold them firm. The thin branches gave the impression of bars on a cage. When Matty found a gap big enough for her to climb through, and then sat inside looking out, the afternoon sun shone in between the branches and made criss-cross shadows across her clothes. She followed the line of the shadows with her fingers as they spread out along her dress, singing softly to herself all the while. She sat here for some time, content, until suddenly a voice broke the silence of the wood, and made Matty jump.

"Hello! Hello, there. What're you doing in there all on your own?"

Matty drew her knees up to her chest and hugged them, and then stared at the source of the voice. A man stood a little way off in the trees. Matty watched as he approached the shelter and bent down to peer in. She drew her knees up even tighter and said nothing. She couldn't get a clear view of the man's face because the branches were in the way, so that he also looked, from Matty's point of view, as if he were in a cage. Still, Matty thought his eyes looked kind. She thought he looked a little bit like her father. He was dressed in a tunic and trousers, and in one hand he carried an axe.

"My name's Seth. What's yours?"

Matty didn't answer.

"Alright. What're you doing hiding in there? You in trouble?"

Matty shook her head to indicate 'no'.

"Well, then. Are you lost?"

Matty shook her head again, and again indicated 'no'.

"It gets cold in these woods, once the sun starts to go round the hill. You coming with me, and we'll find your mother?"

Matty thought about Thea for the first time since she'd watched her trying to hang out the dress in the wind. Had Thea sent Seth to find her? Matty wasn't sure what to do, and now she felt frightened. Her bottom lip trembled and Seth saw that she was about to burst into tears.

"Come on. You don't need to be afraid. Come on out and we'll get you sorted."

Seth held out his hand to support his invitation. Matty felt reassured and she climbed out of the shelter.

"I'm going back to the village now. D'you want to come with me?"

Matty nodded.

"This way, then."

Seth gently took Matty's hand and started to lead her up the hill. He seemed to know where he was going, and the journey didn't seem as challenging as Matty's earlier climb. Matty looked around as she walked. Shouldn't she be going back down the hill? Isn't that the tall tree she passed on the way up? Then Matty looked up ahead in the direction they were walking. Or is that the tall tree she passed, up ahead? Matty was confused, and she followed Seth as he climbed upwards, because she didn't know what else to do.

Seth chatted to Matty as they strolled upwards.

"I bet you're hungry, eh? We'll find you something to eat when we get back."

"My mother will feed me when I get home," Matty thought, but didn't say this out loud.

Quicker than Matty expected, they reached the summit. Seth stood for a moment, to catch his breath, and Matty took the opportunity to look across the valley below. The view stretched as far as she could see, and below her, in the fields, lay the village. Matty felt comfortable with the idea of going home; the trick had been fun but now she wanted to get back to her parents. She scanned the village and tried to make out her garden, the familiar washing line and the huge dog. She searched and searched, and couldn't see anything that looked familiar. However, Seth seemed so reassuring as he squeezed her tiny hand in his and started to walk forwards and downwards, that Matty was certain he was taking her home, and that he knew how to get there even if she did not.

*   *   *

After about half-an-hour of careful climbing down the steep hill, Seth led Matty across the field and into the village. Matty looked around, hoping to see her mother or her father, or both. Instead, as she walked along by Seth's side, people stared. A group of children were playing in the centre of the village, and they stopped their game to watch as Matty walked past. People came out of their gardens or stopped their chores as Seth continued through the village to a larger house at the end. He stopped at the door and a man appeared. He was middle-aged, with kind eyes that twinkled when he smiled. He stared at Matty for a moment, and Matty stared back. She was a pitiful sight. Her clothes were covered in mud, and torn where she'd caught them on branches and the sharp edges of stones. Her hair was bedraggled and knotted, stuck in clumps to her head. The man continued to inspect Matty for a while, and then spoke.

"Well, Seth. What have you got here?"

"Found her up on the hill, in the children's den."

The man bent down to Matty's level. He looked at her kindly.

"What's your name?"

Matty stared at him.

"How did you get to be up on the hill?"

"I ran away."

"Where from?"

"My mother."

The man stood up again.

"It's getting late. She can stay the night here, with Maria and I. Then we'll think about what to do."

Seth nodded his agreement and pushed Matty forwards.

"Come on, then," the man continued, waiting for her. Matty followed him into the house.

Inside the house was dark and dingy, but when Matty's eyes got used to the darkness, she saw that it wasn't that different to her own house. There was a bright fire burning in the hearth, and a large pot of water boiling over it. The large kitchen table was set for the evening meal, with the wooden cups and cutlery and metal plates that they used at home. The familiar scene made Matty relax a little, and when a woman in a black dress turned from the fire and smiled at her, Matty smiled back.

"Hello? What have you got here, Joseph?" the woman whispered.

"A child, Maria, who's come to stay the night."

Maria held out her hand and Matty stepped forward.

"She hasn't told anyone her name yet," Joseph continued.

"That's alright," Maria whispered. "All in good time. Now - shall we get you cleaned up?"

Ten minutes later Matty sat in a tin bath, full to the brim with water heated over the open fire. She said nothing as Maria gently cleaned her up and teased the tangles from her hair. She continued to watch in silence as Maria disappeared into another room and came back with a pile of clean clothes. She lifted Matty out of the bath, dried her down and dressed her in a pair of child's leather boots, a dress and a warm woollen shawl. Matty looked down at herself, then up at Maria. She wondered why the clothes fitted her so well, and felt more confused. Was she at home..........or not?

Maria bent down so that she could look Matty in the eye.

"Now, my dear, can you tell me your name?"

"Matty."

Maria smiled at the whispered reply.

"What a pretty name. And now, Matty, are you hungry?"

Matty nodded a 'yes'.

Maria led Matty to a large wooden kitchen table and helped her up onto an equally large chair. On the table was a plate with bread, cheese and fruit. Maria pushed the plate in front of Matty and watched as she ravenously ate everything. When Matty had finished eating, Maria picked her up, cradled her in her arms and sang a song. Matty allowed herself a tiny smile, and gazed all around her as Maria took her into the room from where she'd produced the clothes. The room turned out to be a tiny bedroom. In the corner stood a child's bed. A small candle burned on a table next to the bed. As Matty looked round, her eyes came to rest on a box full of wooden dolls and animals. Matty smiled. She only had a couple of dolls at home. The box was full to the brim with new playthings. Maria noticed the direction of Matty's gaze and carried her over to the box.

"It's time for you to go to sleep now, Matty. Do you want to take any toys to bed with you?"

Matty pulled the two largest dolls she could find out of the box and held them close. Maria smiled.

"Always the same favourites," she said mysteriously.

She tucked Matty under a heavy wool blanket and sat on the bed.

"Who's bedroom is this?" Matty whispered.

Maria seemed to think for a moment.

"Why, it's your bedroom, of course."

Matty glanced round again. This was definitely not her bedroom. It was too cheerful and friendly to be her room.

"Goodnight, dear Matty," Maria whispered, as she gently kissed the top of Matty's head. Matty watched as Maria blew out the candle, left the room and closed the door firmly behind her. As her eyes grew accustomed to the dark, and she could see the room lit up by the moonlight that shone through the window, Matty felt the fatigue of the day's events overcome her, and she fell instantly asleep. Later that night, Matty woke to the sound of raised voices. She sat up in bed and listened. She knew it wasn't the voices of her parents, and then she gradually remembered where she was. Matty knew that the bright light shining through underneath the bedroom door came from an oil lamp, and now and then the beam of light was broken, suggesting that someone was pacing up and down next door. She tried to catch what they were saying.

In the kitchen, it was Joseph who was pacing up and down. He had arrived back from his business in the village, to find that Maria had all too easily become attached to the little girl that Seth had found on the hill.

"What are you thinking of, Maria? We have to find out where the girl is from, and take her home. I said she could stay tonight."

"Yes, I know, Joseph, but perhaps she isn't lost. Perhaps she is a gift for us, because we never had another child of our own, in all these years, as if we were only allowed to have Leah. I think Matty is our new child."

"Don't be ridiculous. How could that be?"

Joseph knew he had to choose his words carefully. He knew his wife had suffered years of depression, and that the wrong handling of this situation would send her into a relapse. Joseph paused before he spoke.

"I don't think it was wise to put her in Leah's clothes, and put her to sleep in her room."

"Oh, don't be stupid, Joseph. I knew I should keep Leah's room as it was, and keep her things. I prayed that there'd be a reason for doing so, and here she is - our Matty."

"Our Matty? The child is not 'our Matty'. Presumably she has parents somewhere else."

"But she said she ran away from her mother. She must be unhappy. She'll be happy here and....."

"No!" Joseph interrupted. "Tomorrow she will go home."

"Where? Where will you take her?"

"She must be from the other village."

"But we can't go there."

"I know," Joseph said quietly, "but we will have to do something. She can't stay here, and she will never replace our Leah. No-one will."

Next door, Matty listened to the raised voices without understanding what they were saying. The voices stopped. Matty heard a door slam, the light in the other room went out and she fell asleep again.

*   *   *

Matty woke next morning to find the sun streaming through the window. She climbed out of bed and walked sleepily into the kitchen. Joseph and Maria were sitting at the table. They both looked across at Matty as she approached.

"Hello, Matty. Look, Joseph, at the little angel waking from her sleep."

Joseph smiled and said nothing. Maria opened her arms to greet Matty, who climbed up onto her lap. There was a long, tense silence.

"If she has to go........."

"Maria."

"No, Joseph, listen. Today is our 'village day'. We are celebrating anyway today, aren't we? No work, and a day of play for everyone."

"Yes, but........"

"So, why can't we let Matty join in our village day, and then at the end of the day we can search for her parents. Who knows, they may appear anyway, just as she did, searching for her."

Joseph looked grim. He could see that Maria was becoming even more attached to the child, and was looking for a way to let her stay another night.

"I don't know what everyone else will say. We haven't consulted anyone."

"But Joseph - you are the leader of our village. Why do you need to consult anyone? And I also thought...."

Joseph's heart became heavy when Maria paused, as if he knew what was coming.

".....I thought that we could dress Matty in some fine clothes, and she can sit at the head of the table by you, as your guest."

"No, no, no!" Joseph shouted. "There are ways to do things. You know that as well as I! The guest for today is Clayton, Jethro's boy. We

66

planned this. It is the boy's turn. We will offend Jethro and his wife if we push Clayton from his special day."

"You can sort this out for me. You are the leader of our village. They will respect you."

Joseph suddenly wished Seth had never found Matty on the hill, but he quickly pushed that thought away and concentrated on appeasing his wife. He turned to look at her. He saw the fire in her eyes, the life force that was driving her in her game of pretend, and he knew he had to explain to Jethro and Clayton how much he had to do this, for her. He loved his wife as he had loved his daughter, and he knew he couldn't bear to see Maria go back to the cold, dull place she'd withdrawn to when Leah died. He had to make Jethro understand.

As the sun hung high overhead, indicating midday, the whole village - every man, woman and child - assembled in the centre, in the place used for celebrations, mourning and debate. The men had spent the morning setting out rows of tables and benches, while the women organised their summer fayre; pheasants, ducks and rabbits cooked in local aromatic herbs, fruit fresh from their own orchards and vegetables from their fields. They were an affluent village and they worked together well.

After every family had assembled and sat down, Joseph and Maria appeared to take their seats at the head of the table. Between them, Matty walked along holding tightly onto Maria's hand. She wore a dress dyed in a mixture of bright colours. A chain of daisies decorated her hair. Everyone watched in silence as she sat down in the space between Joseph and Maria. Joseph looked across the group of villagers.

"Today is our celebration day, one of our village days. As you know, we were blessed with the company of this child, Matty, who was found on the hill. If she had not been found, she may have perished up there, all alone. We will ensure her safe return to her parents, but until then we are honouring her visit by placing her at the head of our table. Please make the child feel welcome. Now, eat, drink and enjoy."

Everyone applauded Joseph's words, and then as one, the crowd broke into feasting, music and dancing that would go on long into the afternoon.

During the celebrations, Matty stayed firmly by Maria's side. She clutched the folds of Maria's dress while she and other women discussed village affairs and cleared up the dishes and plates from the tables. Suddenly Matty felt a sharp poke in her back. She turned round and saw a group of children staring at her. They seemed to range in age between four years old and ten, and were led by the tallest boy, who stood at their head. It was he who'd poked her in the back.

"Come on. Come and play," he said.

Matty looked up at Maria, who was busy talking and didn't notice

Matty as she let go of her dress and walked over to the group of children. They laughed and smiled at her, and Matty wasn't sure what to do; she had never played with other children before, never been allowed out of the garden, always amused herself.

Suddenly the group of children broke up and shot off in different directions.

"Come on! Catch us if you can!" they all shouted back to Matty.

She laughed too and ran after them. The children ran off and away from the villagers, heading for a nearby field. They coaxed Matty after them, calling teasingly to her, and then ducking and diving as she reached out to touch them. Finally the children stopped trying to escape, and instead they crowded round Matty, still led by the tall boy. They stared in silence at Matty, and she stared back. Suddenly Matty felt afraid. She was probably the youngest and smallest child there, and they seemed to be pushing inwards, shutting her in the centre of their sinister circle. They all looked at the tall boy, who stepped forward.

"My name's Clayton," he said. "It was my turn to sit with Joseph today, at the head of the table. You took that away from me."

Matty was confused, unaware that she'd done anything at all to affect the day's proceedings.

"You have to be punished for doing that to me," Clayton continued.

Matty understood the word 'punished' well enough. She watched as Clayton picked up a stick - a long, thin switch - and stepped towards her. She saw her chance, pushed through a gap between two of the younger children before they could grab at her, and was off across the field.

In a panic, Matty had no plan, but she found herself heading for the hill again, just as she had when she'd run away from Thea the day before. Matty stopped momentarily to kick off her heavy boots, and then she ran as fast as she could. She reached the tree line at the bottom of the hill and looked back. The group of children were behind her, and catching up on her fast. She headed up the hill, repeating the climb from the previous day, and snatching at tree roots and rocks to pull herself up faster. She reached the summit and headed down the other side without stopping. She had to get home.

Matty ran, slipped and fell down the other side of the hill. When she looked back, the children were still fast behind her, still gaining. When Matty came across the shelter made from tree branches, where Seth had found her, she climbed inside, pulled her knees up close, and felt safe. She noticed that it was beginning to get dark as she panted hard, trying to get her breath back. She hoped that the children wouldn't see her in the hideout, and would run on past instead.

Matty's hopes proved futile. Her hideout belonged to this group of wild things. It was their den, their territory, and it was the first place they looked in when they arrived in the clearing. Matty could only watch, trapped, as Clayton led the others towards the den, walking slowly like hunters stalking their prey. Matty did not understand that that was exactly what she had become.

When the children reached the den, they walked round and round it, slowly and methodically, staring in with eyes full of dark intent. Matty turned her head this way and that, trying to keep an eye on everyone and what they were doing. Eventually the children stopped and all looked at Clayton, their leader. He smiled a horrible, knowing, evil smile and then he picked up a small branch, took a small sharp knife from his pocket and carved the end into a sharp point. Now he walked towards Matty, spear in hand, like some sort of ancient warrior. One by one the other children used Clayton's knife to carve themselves a weapon of their own. And now here they were, surrounding Matty, who sat isolated and alone, with no-one to take her side.

Matty felt only the first sharp jab, and then everything went numb. Something stabbed her from behind, deep in her lower back. Instinctively she shot forward away from the threat, and turned to see the look of triumph on a little girl's face. Matty felt the back of her dress, where it seemed wet and sticky, and when she pulled her hand back she saw it was covered in thick, congealed blood. The horror of the moment would have washed over her to create a feeling of total terror, but there was no time. In an instant she was attacked by a second child, then another, then another, until the whole group was on her, squeezing their sharpened sticks through the bars of the den, coming at Matty from all directions so that there was nowhere to hide.

The children whooped and cheered as the sticks penetrated Matty's skin over and over, and she bled profusely from a hundred tiny wounds. Then the mood changed, the children became subdued and still, and Matty felt herself become faint. She curled up on the ground, now wet underneath her and coloured red by a seeping darker and darker bloodstain. The children stared in silence, and then they heard a noise in the trees. Looking back, they saw familiar faces from their own village, people carrying flaming torches against the growing twilight, and approaching them with looks of grim concern. Their own parents were there, with Joseph, Maria and Seth, and suddenly the children woke as if from a trance, and shot away down the hill. As the villagers watched their shameful offspring disappear, there was a second sound of rustling in the trees across from them, and Jacob led his own group into the clearing.

Both groups of villagers stood frozen to the spot, staring at each other as strangers do, knowing exactly who each other was and yet knowing no-one. They looked in disbelief at the tiny, bloodied mess which lay pitifully in the wooden cage. Suddenly, the silence was broken by two simultaneous howls of despair. It took the others a moment to realise firstly that the cries were human, and secondly that they came from both Matty's mother, and from Maria - the 'second mother' who had wanted Matty for herself. Joseph held Maria back at a respectful distance, and everyone watched as Jacob approached the cage, the horror of the terrible event becoming clearer with every step. They continued to watch as Jacob lifted Matty's limp body out of the cage and placed her in Thea's arms, whereupon the couple's knees seemed to bend collectively and they fell to the ground in a commotion of grief and guilt. The others from both villages looked on in silence, unable to comfort and unable to help. Those who had known Jacob and Thea for years, and had often spoken of their 'weird child' behind their backs, knew that the couple's anguish was caused by their realisation of, in death, the absolute value of their only child.

The men amongst each group, being more practical, indicated to the women that they should step away to a distance and leave the family alone for a time. As they did so, turning quietly and walking away into the trees, there was a sudden change in the mood of the weeping and wailing which forced them to turn back.

For what was occurring here? No longer tears of grief and sorrow, but shouts and cries of joy came from Jacob and Thea. How so? As everyone turned, they could not quite believe their eyes; there was Matty, shaky and confused, looking dreadful in her bloodstained clothes, but getting to her feet and looking around her as one woken from a terrible dream. They watched as Matty looked and recognised her parents, and then fell on them to hug them both, as if nothing had happened. Thea's eyes glanced up to the sky in sheer relief, while Jacob could only stare, confused and afraid. Thea held Matty tight and laughed across to her husband.

"I can't believe this. I can't. What a miracle! I didn't tell you before, because I was afraid of what it meant, but this is why Matty was given her gift, so she could save herself! She was given it to save herself on this day! Oh, thank you! Thank you!"

Jacob stared at Thea as if she'd gone completely mad.

"What are you talking about, woman? What gift? Tell me. What do you mean?"

The others had gathered around now, intrigued and afraid.

"Matty is so special, Jacob, and it's taken this to make us see. She's a healer, Jacob, like in the days of the old ones."

"What?"

"I didn't tell you, but I knew, because she burned her hand in the fire and it healed up, right in front of my eyes. And she told me that she cut her finger in the garden and it healed straight away. It made me afraid, so I didn't tell you."

"But what will this mean?"

Joseph stepped forward now and spoke to Jacob for the first time.

"It means you have a special daughter, one that you must nurture and teach and look after. You've been given a sign and a chance to do this."

He looked across at Maria and looked very sad.

"Please don't waste it."

Matty squeezed free of Thea's tight grip and looked up at her parents.

"Can I go back to my real bed now?"

Everyone smiled, and Jacob picked Matty up in his arms. The two groups of people looked at each other now, unsure what to do or say.

"I thought I had been given a daughter, because I lost my own," Maria said quietly. "But I know I can't keep her."

There was a pause. Everyone was thinking of the old story, and the right people and the wrong people who lived on either side of the hill, and had fallen out with each other years ago, over something nobody could remember. Jacob looked around at his own group of friends.

"Perhaps all this happened to Matty for a reason. Perhaps she was meant to get lost to help us to meet. If you like, you could come to us after the snows melt, and celebrate the new spring with us."

People murmured a cautious approval to each other. Joseph stepped forward and held out his hand to Jacob, who took it warmly and the two men shook hands on the arrangement.

"We will come, and we will look forward to it."

Now Maria stepped forward and stroked Matty's hair.

"Goodbye, sweetheart. See you in the spring."

*   *   *

The following spring, warm weather came early. The snows on the high surrounding hills and in the valleys between quickly melted, followed by the emerging buds and flowers that announced the world's new start. On a bright spring morning, with this new world growing all around, the people from Matty's village gathered on the outskirts nearest the high hill, to await their guests from the other side; guests invited in such trauma and such a long time before.

"Would they even come?" People murmured their thoughts aloud amongst themselves. Was Matty's terrible experience a sign that they should be doing more to live and work together, putting old feuds behind them? Then, as people crowded together with their tense misgivings and hopeful expectations, someone standing at the front called out and pointed. Everyone looked in the same direction as one, and they saw them - the people from the other side of the hill - gradually emerging from the trees. Now one or two, now a family, then a larger group, until a procession of brightly-clad figures snaked down the hill and across the open ground. The procession carried with it bundles of food, drink and gifts. The women and girls wore flowers braided in their hair, while the men and boys had made efforts to wear their brightest shirts.

When the procession was close enough to see better, Jacob and Thea saw that Joseph and Maria were out at the front, leading the other villagers, and then they both gasped in surprise when they realised that the bundle Maria was carrying was not any food or drink. It was a baby, a tiny newborn baby! When the procession stopped and the stragglers caught up, the two groups of villagers gathered and watched each other, without at first saying anything.

"Where's Matty?" Maria suddenly shouted. "We want to see Matty."

Thea bent down and gently pushed her daughter through the crowd. Shyly Matty stepped forward as Maria called again, and she walked towards Maria when she beckoned warmly to her. Maria bent down to show Matty the baby.

"Look, Matty. This is my baby. Her name is Alia. I think you helped me, Matty, to make this baby, just like you helped yourself up on the hill. When I held you close you made me well."

Matty didn't really understand. She bit her lip nervously and shuffled about. Joseph ruffled Matty's hair and then looked around.

"And now your invitation to celebrate the new spring is also a celebration for our new daughter, for Alia, a child we thought we would never see."

Everyone burst into cheers and clapped Joseph's speech, and the two groups of villagers, as if being given a sign to move, suddenly fell on each other, shaking hands, hugging, slapping each other on the back, and offering to help to carry the various wares that had been brought along. As one crowd now, they set off through the village towards the square, to set everything up for their spring feast. Only Jacob and Joseph hung back, watching Matty walk by Thea's side as Thea chatted to Maria. As they watched, Thea affectionately took Matty's hand and drew her nearer to her. Joseph smiled.

"People will come," he said quietly.

"I know," Jacob replied.

"Your child has a rare gift. You must take care of her."

Joseph set off after the others, and Jacob could only nod in agreement as he stood watching the happy scene. Stood so far back and alone, no-one saw the tears in his eyes; tears of guilt, relief and pride.

A High Windy Place

Sally's daughter Megan lived in Australia with her husband and three children. A retired teacher, and recently widowed, Sally had spent the last three months resisting all her daughter's attempts to get her to join them there.

"I'm fine. Stop worrying," she moaned in yet another phone call.

"I know, Mum, but maybe it hasn't hit you yet, that Dad's really gone. I would feel much more settled if you were here with us."

"I know, dear, and I appreciate your concern, but I know what I'm doing. If I change my mind, I'll let you know."

Sally couldn't help feeling cross with her daughter at times. She knew that Megan only meant well, but honestly, did she think she was stupid? Frank had been ill for months. She had nursed him. She didn't need it to 'hit her', the realising he'd gone. She'd been there.

She and Frank had talked for hours about how she'd cope, and that's what she was doing. First, Sally sold the large family house and bought a small cottage in the same village. Rose Cottage. It was a quirky little place, very old, steeped in history, the estate agent had said, although exactly what that history was, Sally hadn't been able to find out. The cottage was just right; old stone walls, roses in the garden, a living room and kitchen downstairs, a bedroom and bathroom upstairs, a cellar below and an attic above. Sally had loved it and put an offer in straight away. Now here she was, in her tiny new home; *her* tiny new home. She was content.

Or so she thought. Sitting alone in the evenings, or waking up in the mornings, she found that she missed Frank more than she expected, and she mulled over Megan's words more than she expected to as well.

"Pull yourself together, girl. You have a plan," she repeated to herself.

There were jobs that needed doing, mostly to undo the previous owner's 'modernising' of the interior. Sally wanted to restore its old-fashioned style. She raked around in the many boxes she'd shoved in the cellar and found a crowbar; this morning's job was to pull up the false laminate flooring in the kitchen and see what was underneath. Sally wasn't disappointed. The previous owners had used their flooring to hide the original floorboards, which were old, with gnarled patterns in the wood, much more beautiful than that modern stuff. Sally smiled as she continued to prise up each row of the new wood, revealing another row of the old.

As her progress across the floor reached the middle of the kitchen, she pulled up the latest piece of laminate and discovered, underneath and set into the floorboard, a metal plate. She looked at it curiously. It was about eight inches square, a tiny metal hatch with a hinge on one side and a slight lip on the other, so you could put your finger in and lift it up. It sat nicely inside a metal surround. Sally was intrigued; someone had obviously gone to the effort of putting it there, but why? It wasn't big enough to let anyone in or out. How strange.

Sally's obvious next move was to lift the plate up and peep in. Below, she could see the vague shadows of the part of the cellar that was immediately below her, but nothing more. No matter how much she craned her neck or leaned over to one side, it was impossible to see any further than just below the gap in the floor. She got back up, found a torch in the kitchen drawer, kneeled back down and shone the torch beam straight into the hole.

A child's face looked back up at her. Sally dropped the torch in fright, the torch disappeared down the hole, and she leapt backwards, sliding along the floor until she felt the security of the kitchen wall behind her. Her knees gave in; she felt the sickness of shock as adrenaline rushed around her system, confusing her. She stared at the hole in the floor for what seemed an eternity, and felt her breath gradually slow as she calmed down. It was a trick of the light, a trick of the shadows; it was anything she could think of, by way of an explanation, except a child looking up at her from her cellar.

When Sally had composed herself fully again, she found a second torch, cautiously knelt at the hole in the floor and looked in. The child's face still stared back. This time Sally tried to stay in control. She studied the child. It was a little boy, aged about eight. He had the huge round eyes that all children have, and a shock of black hair. For a moment, he and Sally gazed at each other in silence, and then bang! Sally lifted the metal plate and slammed it firmly back in place, shutting the child back in the darkness. All that night, Sally tossed and turned in bed. She couldn't escape the child's face looking up at her, calm, patient, expectant. When sleep finally came, she only dreamed about him instead. In the morning, she sat up in bed with a cup of tea and wondered what to do next. Should she leave the metal plate firmly shut, and never open it again? What else could she do? Should she speak to the child and see what she could find out? Sally realised that if she accepted the one thing which frightened her, she could then decide what to do. She let herself face the fact that the child's face was tinged with blue, his lips looked cold. Yes, he was certainly dead. In her cellar.

Later that morning, after much consideration, Sally walked down the wooden staircase that led to the cellar. She looked around, not sure what she was looking for, and it was only then that she noticed something that she'd missed before; the cellar was not as long as the house. She walked from one end of the cellar to the other. Fifteen paces. She walked and counted again, to be sure, and then upstairs, she walked from the front door, where the entrance to the cellar lay, right to the other end of the house. Twenty-five paces. She did this walk again as well, to be sure. Twenty-five paces. The horror of the situation crept in. The child had been walled up in her cellar. Sally decided that she needed a brandy, and she poured a straight one. She sat at the kitchen table and realised that, more than feeling frightened, she was angry. Who would wall a child up in a cellar? It was outrageous, cruel. Two more brandies and Sally was full of Dutch courage. She lifted the metal plate in the floor, firmly this time, and shone the torch in. The child looked back at her.

"What's your name?" she asked.

"Joseph," he replied. "What's yours?"

"Sally. Why are you in my cellar, Joseph?"

"I don't know."

"How long have you been there?"

"Don't know. A long time, I think."

Sally didn't know what to do next, never having been in this situation before. Joseph took the lead.

"Can you let me out?"

Sally was confused. Why did she have to let him out? Couldn't he just get out? Isn't that what ghosts did?

"I'll have to think about that," she replied, and immediately regretted her words. They sounded uncaring and unkind. She looked down at Joseph.

"I'm sorry, I have to go."

This time she didn't close the metal plate over the hole.

For the rest of that day, Sally considered her dilemma. How could she let Joseph out? What would it mean if she did? Would letting him out be the right thing to do, or would she regret it? How would she regret it? Is he an evil spirit, trapped for a reason? Or is he the innocent victim of someone else's evil plan? Sally would have laughed at the questions she had to ask herself, if they weren't so serious. Eventually she made her decision. She would knock down the wall in the cellar.

Two days later, Jim arrived. Jim was an old man who'd lived in the village all his life. Everyone asked him to do their odd jobs. He looked at the wall in the cellar.

"Easy," he muttered, and took a sledgehammer to it.

Sally watched Jim's quick progress. Half an hour later, the wall was down. In readiness, Sally had found her old camping lamp, which gave off a much wider beam than a torch. She carried it as she and Jim stood in the new space. It was completely empty, except for the original torch that she'd dropped down the hole, which sent a long beam along the cellar floor. Jim picked the torch up, turned it off and passed it to Sally.

"You'll have a bit more space now," he said, matter-of-factly.

"Yes. You got the job done really quickly. Thanks. I thought it might have taken ages."

"Why? It was only a plasterboard stud wall."

"Yes," replied Sally, "Only I expected it to be very old. You know, solid stone."

"Actually, I remember when this wall was put up," Jim said, looking around.

"Really?"

Sally wanted to know more.

"Why was it put up?"

"The owners at the time, they were digging out the floor, to tidy it up, like. I think they were going to convert the cellar into a proper room, you know, a play room or something."

"Go on," said Sally, suddenly full of dread.

"They found some bones when they were digging. Human bones. A child's bones."

Sally took a deep breath.

"What happened then?"

"Well, the bones were sent off for tests, like, to see how old they were and stuff like that. I don't think they knew whose bones they were. Afterwards they were buried in the churchyard up the road there, but there was no name to put on the headstone, so it just says 'A child found in the cellar at Rose Cottage', or something like that."

Jim looked at Sally.

"I didn't like to scare you, so I didn't mention it before."

Sally laughed nervously.

"So, do you know why there's a hole in the kitchen floor?"

"No idea. Show me."

Back upstairs in the kitchen, Jim peered down through the hole in the floor. He seemed intrigued, but that was all.

"He can't see him," Sally thought to herself. "He can't see Joseph."

Twenty minutes later, after tea and biscuits and with cash in his pocket, Jim was off down the path. As Sally watched him go, she felt a weight off her shoulders. Jim didn't see anything; the boy was gone. Smiling to herself at a job well done, no matter how weird, she closed and locked the door and turned to go back to the kitchen. She jumped in fright as she turned. There was Joseph, standing in the doorway of the kitchen, staring at her. Same huge eyes, same shock of black hair. He stood barefoot and was dressed only in a pair of ragged trousers. The strange paleness of his tiny body was even more pronounced in the light. She stared back, unsure about what to do.

"I'm hungry," Joseph suddenly said.

"Come on, then," Sally replied.

Sally watched as Joseph ate everything she put in front of him. She was mildly amused at his appetite, remembering how her own children ate healthily and heartily all the time. She also kept reminding herself that this was a very strange situation to be in; feeding a child she's just rescued from an underground prison.

When he'd eaten enough, Joseph started exploring the house. Sally had decided not to ask him any more searching questions, since his answers to her last ones had seemed vague, so instead she indulged him, following him as he searched every room.

"Who's this?" he asked of her family photos on the windowsill in her bedroom.

"That's my daughter Megan, her husband Mike. These are my grandchildren. Sophie is the eldest. She's nine. Then Eliza is six, and Jake is three."

There was a silence in the room, and then Joseph suddenly burst into tears. Sally didn't know whether to reach out to the weeping child, and decided not to.

"Whatever's the matter, Joseph?"

"I want to play with them. They look so happy."

"Well, I'm afraid neither you nor I can play with them. They live on the other side of the world, in Australia."

"Where's that?"

Sally remembered that she had a globe on top of the dresser in the kitchen. Downstairs, she climbed up to get it, while Joseph watched, and placed it on the table. Joseph listened, fascinated, while she showed him where they themselves were, and where Australia was, and exactly where Megan and her family lived.

"Why don't you live there with them?" he asked.

He looked directly at Sally, and she knew what it was that unnerved her. It was his searching eyes, the fixed stare that made her feel uncomfortable.

"Well, my home is here. They used to live here as well, but they moved. Actually, they want me to go there too."

When Joseph seemed satisfied with her explanation, he turned away from Sally to look around the room.

"I'm tired," he suddenly said.

"I can make up a bed in the living room, if you like."

Sally sat in the armchair and watched Joseph. She'd tucked him up under a quilt, because he'd asked her to. Then she'd explained what the television was, since he'd asked, and they sat together watching the children play in one of Megan's home videos. Eventually Joseph fell asleep, and Sally went up to bed too. She contemplated on her weird day. Was this really happening? When Sally came downstairs next morning, Joseph was sitting up on the sofa. He looked at her with that same fixed, determined stare.

"Do you know a high windy place?" he asked, firmly.

Sally thought for a moment.

"Yes, I do."

"Will you show me?"
"Alright."

Joseph sat in the front seat, next to Sally, as they drove in silence. Sally wondered what he made of the car, and of all the other things he could see as they travelled along. She planned to take Joseph to the Kymin, a high viewpoint near to where she lived. Eventually they turned off the main road and drove along the road that wound round and round, up and up to the top. As they drove higher, the view expanded before them. Sally parked the car. There was no-one else about, and she led Joseph to the edge of the viewpoint. The wind blew fiercely and whipped her coat around her. Once at the edge, they looked out in silence at the view, at the clouds blowing rapidly across the sky, at the world going on below them, reaching away into the distance. Joseph slipped his hand into hers. Sally looked down at him, realising that this was the first time she'd touched him. He felt cold and the realisation sent a shiver across her spine.

"You should go to Australia," Joseph said calmly.
"But what about you?" Sally replied, confused.
"You don't have to worry about me. Do the right thing for you."
"Yes, but........" Sally started.
"I'm dead."

Joseph looked at her. They were holding hands very tightly. Suddenly the wind lifted Joseph up off the ground. He said nothing, only stared at Sally as she held on as tight as she could. Sally struggled against the force of a wind that suddenly seemed stronger, a wind that pulled Joseph up into the air in front of her, but seconds later Joseph's hand was wrenched from her own, and he was gone. She watched, helpless, as he was whipped away by the force of the wind, tossed around in the air and carried off into the distance. Joseph looked back all the time, back at Sally, at the person who'd set him free.

"No!" Sally called out after him, without knowing why.

*　　　　　*　　　　　*

Six months later, Sally closed the door of Rose Cottage for the last time. The estate agent was waiting in his car out in the road. As she handed him the keys, he smiled.

"No regrets?"
"No," Sally replied. "Not now."
"Well, have a good flight, won't you, and good luck in Australia."
"Thanks."

Sally waved to the estate agent as he drove away. She had a bit of time before the taxi came to take her to the airport, and she had one last job to do. The cemetery was at the other end of the village. Sally strolled through the gate, a huge bunch of flowers in her hand.

She found the grave she was looking for quickly, for this was not the first time she'd been here. In a quiet corner of the children's section, Sally read, for the last time, the headstone that simply said:

'A tiny child
found in the cellar
at Rose Cottage,
known only to God'

She laid the flowers down on top of the grave.

"I've arranged for Jim to keep fresh flowers here for you, Joseph. I couldn't tell anyone about you. No-one would believe me, would they? But I want to thank you for helping me to make my decision."

Sally sat in silence. For a moment she expected Joseph to appear, hold out his hand, speak to her. Instead, there was nothing, except for the wind whistling through the tall yew trees. Sally smiled.

Three days later, Sally had to smile again. Megan and Mike had bought a new house, to accommodate her joining them. Set up on the top of a hill on the edge of Sydney, they'd called it 'A High Windy Place'.